THE LAST DUCHESS

Praise for The Last Duchess *from Lovereading4kids.co.uk reviewers:*

'A thrilling tale jam-packed with excitement, adventure and mysteries . . . you are sure to love this book if you are into adventures'
Kitty, age 9

'Full of mischief, mystery and crime'
Holly, age 13

'I would have kept reading this book all night if it wasn't for my mum and dad' Amina, age 10

'A gripping tale of a mystery, secrets and friendship' Amelie

'An exciting and intriguing read . . . full of action and suspense' Sidney, age 13

'The best book that I have r
while. I absolutely loved it!'

THE LAST DUCHESS

LAURA POWELL

A SILVER SERVICE MYSTERY

ILLUSTRATED BY SARAH GIBB

MACMILLAN CHILDREN'S BOOKS

First published 2017 by Macmillan Children's Books
an imprint of Pan Macmillan
20 New Wharf Road, London N1 9RR
Associated companies throughout the world
www.panmacmillan.com

ISBN 978-1-5098-0890-8

1 3 5 7 9 8 6 4 2

A CIP catalogue record for this book is available from
the British Library.

Printed and bound by CPI Group (UK) Ltd, Croydon CR0 4YY

For Ali

Upstairs, Downstairs

The Butler

The butler is the principal male servant. His duties include arranging the dining table, carving the meat, serving the wine and attending to the needs of the family and their guests in the dining and drawing rooms. The silverware, cellars and pantries are in his charge.

The Housekeeper

The housekeeper is the principal female servant, and second in command to the butler. She is in charge of the accounts, the tradesmen's bills, the orderly running of the house and the provision of general supplies. She is also responsible for the servants' quarters.

The Valet

The valet attends the master of the household. His duties include keeping his master's wardrobe in order, preparing his bath, shaving him and tidying his dressing room.

The Lady's Maid

The lady's maid waits on the mistress of the household, assisting with her dress and toilette, washing the most delicate items of her wardrobe and using her dressmaking skills to create and repair clothes. In addition, the lady's maid prepares beauty lotions and styles her mistress's hair.

The Footman

The footman sets the table for meals and assists the butler, answers the door and attends to various other tasks in the house, such as lighting candles and lamps, polishing silver and cleaning shoes and boots.

The Housemaids

There are several housemaid positions, including parlour maids, chambermaids and laundry maids. Each has their own set of duties, such as lighting fires, bringing up hot water for washing, emptying and cleaning chamber pots, cleaning all the public rooms of the house, making beds, brushing carpets and beating rugs, and washing clothes and linen.

The Cook

The cook is responsible for the kitchen and the provision of meals. She will not do any general cleaning, and her ingredients will mostly be prepared for her by her staff.

The Kitchen Maids

The duties of the kitchen and scullery maids include lighting the kitchen fires early in the morning and cleaning the kitchen and its utensils for the cook's use throughout the day.

Additional Servants

If there are children in the house, they will be attended to by a **nurse** and **nursery maids**. The **hall-boy** waits on the other servants, runs errands and – if there is no **bootboy** – cleans the shoes of the household. The **coachman** supervises the stables and drives the coach, while the **groom** and **stable boy** look after the horses. Other outdoor servants are **groundsmen** and **gardeners**.

A Warning

I must caution you against taking up such books as would not only take up your time unprofitably, but might also tend to corrupt your principles, and make you dissatisfied with your condition. I mean novels, tales and romances, which have led many a girl to ruin . . .

J. Bulcock, *The Duties of a Lady's Maid*
(London: C. Smith, 1825)

CHAPTER ONE

The perfect servant is an invisible one.

Pattern was one of these. She was so quiet, so small and shadowy, that it was easy to forget she was even in the room. Her quick hands would go about their business – tending and mending, polishing and pinning – apparently with no effort at all. And when she was done, she would melt into the background like a well-trained ghost.

Pattern had only just turned thirteen, but she was going to go far.

This, at least, was the general opinion within Mrs Minchin's Academy of Domestic Servitude. For Pattern had other talents too: a knack for getting even the toughest stains out of linen; darning that was almost as invisible as the rest of her. No button or hairpin had ever gone missing in her care. Her bonnet-trimming was a joy to behold, and having progressed to Advanced Hair-Dressing, she had perfected the art of curling ringlets with hardly any trouble at all.

Even so, Mrs Minchin was somewhat taken aback to be informed that Pattern's services were required by Her Royal Highness Arianwen Eleri Charlotte Louise, Grand Duchess of Elffinberg.

'But . . . forgive me . . . are there no suitable lady's maids in Elffinberg?' she enquired of the noble personage in her parlour. If it were not for the difference in dress, Mrs Minchin looked the more likely aristocrat, with her prim, thin face and haughty eyebrows, whereas Baroness von Bliven had the stoutness and redness of a no-nonsense cook. But the Baroness's eyes were watery, and her hands trembled, and Mrs Minchin had to strain to hear her voice.

'Her Royal Highness has rejected the most likely candidates. It is therefore time to look further afield. As her godmama, I have taken it upon myself to pursue the matter, as a personal favour to the Grand Duchess.'

'I quite understand, Your Ladyship,' said Mrs Minchin, even though none of this made a particle of sense. 'My only concern is that Pattern is a little, ahem, *young* for such an elevated role. Surely one of this year's graduates, a grown girl of sixteen—'

'None of your other girls is of Elffish blood.'

This, Mrs Minchin had to admit, was true.

'Pattern may be young for her position,' said the Baroness, in between painful coughs, 'but then so is the Grand Duchess. In any case, I would be most grateful for your assistance. I need hardly say I expect your utmost discretion in the matter.'

'Naturally,' said Mrs Minchin, with her most ingratiating smile. In fact, this came as a bitter blow.

She had already been picturing *By Royal Appointment* written in gold letters above her door. 'I will tell Pattern the good news directly.'

Pattern did not know which was the more shocking part of the announcement: that she was to be a lady's maid a good seven years ahead of time, or that she was travelling overseas to work for foreign royalty, or that she wasn't a true Englishwoman, after all.

Pattern was chiefly a 'waif and stray'. Her parents had been drowned at sea. A mere baby, Pattern had been found floating in her cradle not far from the wreckage of their boat. She and a couple of the surviving crew members were picked up by a passing cargo ship, whose owner raised enough funds for the child to be sent to one of the more respectable London orphanages, and from there placed in Mrs Minchin's Academy.

Now, however, she learned that the drowned boat had been full of Elffish immigrants, though which of these were her mother and father was unknown. So was her real name. She had been given the surname Pattern by the matron of the orphanage, who had neglected to provide anything else to go with it. It hardly mattered. On entering service, it was customary for a maid to exchange her original name for something plain and easy to remember, like Sarah or Ellen or Prue. So although some might celebrate the title 'Royal Highness' above all things, what Pattern truly envied was the poetry of 'Arianwen Eleri Charlotte Louise'. What luxury, to have not one Christian name, but four!

No hint of such outlandish thoughts was visible during her interview in Mrs Minchin's parlour. 'Yes, ma'am', 'No, ma'am', and 'Thank you, ma'am' was all that meekly passed her lips.

'You are an extraordinarily lucky girl,' said Mrs Minchin in conclusion. Even she was surprised by how quietly Pattern had taken the news. 'I hope you are sensible of your good fortune, and that you will work very hard to be worthy of it.'

'Yes, ma'am. Thank you, ma'am.'

As she closed the parlour door behind her, however, Pattern was not entirely sure of how lucky she felt. She

would not miss the Academy, with its scratchy brown uniforms and draughty dormitory, or the jostling, jealous girls. But London's soot-stained skyline was the only horizon she knew. The idea of a world beyond it seemed almost as fanciful as her sudden promotion to Royal Servitude.

It was now nearly time for supper, and most of her fellow students were trying to warm themselves before the feeble fire in the refectory. Pattern picked up her work basket and went to join a group of three winding wool by the door.

'I am to travel abroad,' Pattern told them, only a little breathlessly. 'I am to work in a great house. I am to leave tomorrow.'

She was not permitted to say more. Really, she should have said nothing at all. But she had to tell somebody *something* of what was about to happen. Perhaps then she would actually believe it.

There was a short pause. Then:

'Well, *I* don't envy you a jot,' sniffed snub-nosed Pol. 'Abroad is full of dirty foreigners, and I wouldn't wish to go there at all.'

'Oh, I don't know. Things happen Abroad that never happen here,' said kind, stupid Jane, whose accomplishments would never progress much beyond potato peeling. 'Battles and revolutions and scandal! I think it must be very exciting.'

'Pattern,' yawned bony Sue, 'is not the kind of person that exciting things happen to. Pattern is as dull and correct as her needlework.'

The other girls tittered. Pattern's expression stayed fixed. She contemplated jabbing Sue's knuckles with a knitting needle, all the while wondering if what she said was true.

Pattern's start in life had certainly been striking – a baby plucked from the towering waves of storm and shipwreck. And here she was, seized by the hand of destiny once more, this time in service to foreign royalty. But perhaps Sue was right, in that it would be better if such dramas befell somebody better suited to them. Someone passionate and picturesque, like the heroines of those romances of which Mrs Minchin

so disapproved. (They gave girls Ideas; and Ideas were very much frowned upon in the Academy of Domestic Servitude.)

A quiet and orderly person could only hope to prosper in a quiet and orderly life. This was what Pattern should work towards. *Then* she would find herself entirely satisfied with her lot.

But having come to this sensible resolution, why did she still have a fiery urge to stab at something with her needles and pins?

On the morning of Pattern's departure, Mrs Minchin offered a great deal of advice, very little of which was to the point, and chiefly related to her own glory days in service to the Countess of Arkminster. Just before parting, she presented Pattern with J. Bulcock's *The Duties of a Lady's Maid: With Directions for Conduct, and Numerous Receipts for the Toilette.*

'I have no doubt,' said Mrs Minchin, in her stateliest manner, 'that you will be a credit to the school.'

Pattern curtsied. In her grey twill travelling dress,

she looked more shadowy than ever. Her eyes were grey too; her face altogether colourless, her mouth small and precise. She wore her light brown hair with a central parting, and looped smoothly above each ear. Her nails were trim, her collar immaculately starched. The very picture, Mrs Minchin thought approvingly, of Attention to Duty.

Pompous old trout, thought Pattern.

The novelty of travel did not last beyond the first day spent in a rattling carriage, squashed up next to the Baroness's own maid, a glum-faced woman with a permanent sniff. At night, she and Pattern shared a bed in a coaching inn, where the woman's sharp elbows and snuffling made rest impossible.

Pattern would have found sleep elusive in any event. The Great Unknown stretched out before her, as

seemingly endless as the dusty road they jolted along. Her only information on their destination came from the encyclopaedia in the Academy's schoolroom. From this, she had learned that the Duchy lay in the rolling forest that the mountains of central Germany thrust out northward to the great European plain. It had been founded by a medieval Welsh Prince, Elffin Pendraig, who had spent several years in exile in Europe before settling there with his followers. The native tongue – Elffish – was consequently derived from German and Welsh, though English had supplanted it in all but the most remote rural communities. There were three principal settlements: the capital city of Elffinheim, the spa-town of Brecon-Baden, and the university town of Myrddinsbruck, high in the mountain ranges of the north. The country was 4,300 square miles, with a population of 390,000. The principal manufacture was porcelain.

Pattern liked facts and figures. She liked to arrange them, tidily, in her head. It made her feel that some of the world's chaos could be put in order after all, in the manner of a well-appointed linen cupboard. Yet what she really wanted was a personal account of the place. Mrs Minchin had impressed upon her that the thirteen-year-old Grand Duchess was also a princess in her own right by virtue of her Welsh ancestry, so she must be very grand indeed. How did Her Royal Highness wear her hair? What colours did she favour in her dress? What were her particular tastes in art, music, pastries, pets?

Would her mistress be kind to Pattern, or pull her hair and pinch her arm, as the older girls did at the Academy?

Would the other servants welcome her, or resent her?

Would she find herself even more alone?

Beware of self-pity, Pattern told herself. Self-pity was a luxury the likes of her could not afford.

The Baroness's maid disapproved of Pattern and so pretended not to understand English whenever she ventured a question. Besides, most of her energies were engaged in nursing her mistress and preparing balms

and syrups for her cough. The Baroness had come to London to visit a famous Harley Street physician, but his treatment had not had the desired healing effect. Her wheezing worsened with each hour on the road.

They reached Elffinberg late on Sunday, after travelling several miles through dense forest. The border was manned by guards in green livery, who sprang out of their sentry-box and presented arms at the carriage's approach. Close by was a small inn, whose landlady sold souvenirs as well as providing lodging. Her wares included Elffish flags, marzipan sweets, and china plates painted with the Grand Duchess's portrait. It depicted a simpering girl-child with pink cheeks and black curls, of the kind found on any chocolate box.

The next morning, Pattern was summoned to the Baroness's bed chamber. There she was informed that the Baroness was too ill to travel on to the royal residence. Pattern must go alone. The Baroness had prepared a letter of introduction for her to give to the Master of the Royal Household, and another for the Grand Duchess. Also, documents attesting to Pattern's parentage, which the Baroness had obtained from the Elffinberg consul in London.

'It was he who advised me of your placement in Mrs Minchin's establishment. This is a small country, and a sheltered one. Secretive, one might say. Very few people visit; even fewer leave. If you were not a compatriot, you would not be permitted to seek employment here.'

The Baroness was still stout and red, but her skin had a sunken, waxy look, and her wheezing was so pronounced that Pattern had to lean close to hear her.

'The Grand Duchess is young – no older than you. Her position means that she has led an isolated life, with few companions her own age and few engagements other than official ones. She is, I regret, not on friendly terms with her uncle and guardian, Prince Leopold. So although my dear Arianwen is the sweetest creature in the world, she is of a somewhat nervous disposition, and prone to strange flights of fancy. In truth, she has taken it into her head that all her servants are spies, in the pay of the Prince, and that her last lady's maid was attempting to poison her.'

Pattern swallowed, and murmured she was very sorry to hear that.

'Do not alarm yourself. As a stranger to the land, Her Royal Highness can hardly suspect *you* of conspiring against her. It may be, too, that your closeness in age will help win her confidence.'

Here the Baroness had to take pause for a prolonged coughing fit. The handkerchief she pressed to her mouth was spotted in blood. 'I was very fond of the Grand Duchess's mother,' she said, once she was somewhat recovered. 'Very fond. I have tried to look out for her child as best I could. My health, however, means I have not been as great a friend as I could wish. Or for as long as I would hope.'

She sighed, and her breath rattled painfully. 'So I ask you to attend to Her Royal Highness's comfort in every way. Not just in the particulars of her toilette, but in promoting her peace of mind.'

Pattern stuttered an attempt at assurance. But the Baroness placed a hand on hers. Her flesh was cold and heavy.

'One does not have to be unduly fanciful,' the Baroness said, 'to know that royal courts are chancy places. So this is my advice to you. Stay aloof from intrigue, attend to your mistress, keep your counsel. *And trust no one.*'

CHAPTER TWO

The country of Pattern's birth was as pretty as a picture book. Under the shadow of the mountain range, its valleys were lush, its forests dark, its rivers silvery. The approach of autumn had only just begun to give the foliage a tawny tint. New white villas peeped out from trees, old thatched cottages huddled by lakes. After the foggy stink of London, the air was sweet and fresh.

Why had her mother and father ever sought to emigrate? The Elffish looked to be a prosperous and plump, contented people. Pattern felt a stab of longing. Here was proof that a taste for adventure was most likely to end in disaster. If only her parents had been satisfied with their lot, she could have had a real home, and a family, in this pleasant place.

As the evening light grew low, the horse and trap approached the jumble of red roofs and grey gables that was the city of Elffinheim. There was a statue of a knight in the main square, a small yet fearsome dragon by his side, and Pattern thought it was St George, before realizing it must be Elffin, the Welsh prince who gave the Duchy its name.

But with her final destination so near at hand, she became too distracted by her conversation with Baroness von Bliven to take much pleasure in the sights around her. In one shaky breath, the Baroness had called her goddaughter nervous and fanciful; in another, she had warned Pattern to trust nobody. If the

Grand Duchess was unstable, paranoid even, and chose to accuse Pattern of some crime . . . what could she do, alone and friendless in a foreign country?

Since she had no other guide, Pattern took out the book given to her by Mrs Minchin, *The Duties of a Lady's Maid*, and turned to the chapter on 'Change of Place'. She read:

> *Never give your ear or your countenance to those malicious gossiping persons who would put you up against your situation, by telling you all manner of stories of the family; for it is a thousand to one that such stories are untrue.*

The Baroness was good-hearted; of that Pattern was sure. Yet she was also very sick, and perhaps her judgement was unsound. Pattern resolved to think no more of plots and poisonings. Nevertheless, as the groom drove the trap through the wrought-iron gates that led to the Castle of Elffinberg, she felt her spirits sink deep into the soles of her sensible boots.

The castle lay at the end of a two-mile-long avenue carved through a pine wood. It was a vast and ugly pile, half Greek temple, half Gothic cathedral. Its ranks of pillars were stained by the droppings of many generations of pigeons, the tiers of windows looked as if they were rarely cleaned, and the plasterwork was cracked and yellowing.

The main portico overlooked an immense cobbled forecourt and a fountain that dribbled water from a tangle of sea horses and mermaids. Pattern – naturally –

was delivered to the back entrance, past stables large enough to house several herds of horses, and into a paved yard where scraps of dead leaves and rubbish swirled. There she was met by a bootboy, who went to fetch a slovenly-looking maid, who went to fetch the Head Housekeeper, who went to fetch the Master of the Household.

All of this took a great deal of time, and Pattern, left to wait on the doorstep like an unwanted parcel, felt most uncomfortable. The Master of the Household, when he finally appeared, looked to have been roused from his tea, for there were crumbs all down his shirt and jam on his collar. He read the Baroness von Bliven's letter slowly and grudgingly. 'I suppose,' he said, even more grudgingly, 'you'd better come in.'

Pattern was passed back into the care of the Head Housekeeper, Mrs Parry, who was small and pursy, with shiny black button eyes. 'My,' she said, on first seeing Pattern, 'but you're a dismal scrap of a thing,' before asking her if England was as wet and dirty as everybody said.

Pattern replied that it was, on occasion.

'Well, I dare say one gets used to it. I doubt you'll be here long enough to get homesick, in any case.'

With these discouraging words, Mrs Parry informed Pattern that the Grand Duchess was indisposed and would not receive her until later that evening – if at all. In the meantime, she was to be given a tour of the service quarters. It appeared that a number of noble personages had apartments within the castle, and that attending to their needs provided employment for half of Elffinheim.

They began in the servants' hall, a draughty dungeon of a place filled with much noise and disorder. From there Pattern was whisked past laundries and larders, sculleries and butteries, pantries and spiceries; rooms for trimming candles, for storing root vegetables, for polishing silver and for blacking boots . . . Bells rang at every moment, from every corner, and people dressed in all manner of shabby uniforms hastened to obey them. It was an underground labyrinth, damp and dim as any cellar, though a great deal more confusing.

Pattern struggled to keep the pace, let alone remember all the information she was so carelessly and quickly given. She could not help but be concerned as to the whereabouts of her luggage, which had been taken off by a bootboy, and she feared the worst as to the tidiness of her hair and the cleanliness of her hands. Everything was so large and elaborate that she felt very small and insignificant indeed, and quite unequal to whatever tasks should be asked of her.

Finally a little page-boy scampered up to whisper in Mrs Parry's ear: the Grand Duchess was ready for them. By now, Pattern's throat was parched, and she was near faint with hunger. But there was no time for refreshment, let alone a moment to wash away the dust of the journey or re-pin her hair. Instead, she followed the rustle of Mrs Parry's skirts up creaking staircases with splintered hand-rails, along limewashed corridors and round cramped corners, through a baize-lined door that swung silently behind them – and into a spacious, well-lit hallway, whose carpet was soft as moss.

The doors to the Grand Duchess's bedchamber

were at the end. It was a room as big as a field, with a four-poster bed as a big as a cottage. The bed was walled with drapes of purple satin suspended from an enormous golden crown near the ceiling. Light glowed from a scattering of candlesticks; every window was shrouded in curtains of dusty plum-coloured velvet. It was stuffy and silent and seemingly deserted.

Mrs Parry advanced upon the giant bed. There was a set of portable steps propped against the end. Mrs Parry paused at their base, head bowed. She gave a small cough.

'Crumpets and crinolines! Am I *never* to have any peace?' exclaimed a peevish voice from within the drapery.

There was a sound of creaking bed-springs and flounced linens. The curtains twitched, and a small sharp face framed by a large white nightcap poked out. The face was scowling.

'It is the Young Person from England, Your Highness,' murmured Mrs Parry.

Her Royal Highness Arianwen Eleri Charlotte

Louise, Grand Duchess of Elffinberg, looked Pattern up and down and curled her lip.

'An English spy! How novel. I suppose they have run out of the native sort.' Then: 'Go away,' she said. 'Go away, both of you, and leave me alone. You make me bilious to my bones.'

CHAPTER THREE

You must recollect there is no place wherever where every thing will be as you wish it, and this ought to make you bear with many little things that are not so agreeable.

J. Bulcock, *The Duties of a Lady's Maid*

Pattern ate a solitary supper in her room. It would have been better to join her fellow servants in the hall, and so begin making the alliances necessary for working life. By rights, she should have been invited to take tea in the housekeeper's sitting room. But although Mrs Parry's offer of a supper-tray might be seen as an indulgence,

its message was clear: Pattern was on her own.

Her attic room was, by virtue of her position, a little way apart from the other maids'. It had a good-sized window and a lockable desk, and the bed was brightened by a patchwork counterpane. It did not take long to unpack her box and arrange her things: three dresses and one smock, two petticoats, two nightgowns, two chemises, four pairs of drawers, two nightcaps, and four pairs of stockings. There was room in the mahogany closet for twice as much.

In spite of such magnificence, Pattern's night was not a comfortable one. It was the first time she had ever slept on her own. She missed the night-time breathing and rustling of the other girls at Mrs Minchin's Academy. Even the snores of Baroness von Bliven's maid would have been welcome. She was a stranger, alone a strange land. The silence and vastness of the castle closed around her, even blacker than the night.

The morning did not bring much cheer. One of the Third Housemaids brought her breakfast, banging down the tray on the desk so that the tea slopped and soaked the bread. She was a red-headed girl of about sixteen, with a saucy tilt to her nose and a snap in her voice.

'You must think very highly of yourself, I'm sure,' she said, without opening or introduction. 'Swanning in here with your hoity-toity English airs, and stealing jobs from under the noses of honest Elffish folk.'

Pattern kept her voice as steady as she was able. 'My family were Elffish-born. I believe that is why the Baroness—'

'Elffish-born? Ha! Now you show yourself to be a fraud as well as a thief, for nobody leaves Elffinberg without the permission of the Ducal Family. It's forbidden.' The girl tossed her head. 'Well, I don't know what trick you pulled on old Bliven, but the joke's on *you*. The GD is a wildcat, make no mistake. She came near to scratching out the eyes of her last maid. And kicked the one before that all the way down the grand staircase.'

'In that case,' said Pattern, very innocently, 'you and your friends must be highly relieved not to have

been selected for the position.'

The maid gave her a hard stare. 'Don't flatter yourself that Her Highness wants you any more than we do. She went to her godmama's sickbed at first light, but as soon as she returns she'll be sure to send you packing. There's folk who say Her Highness is cracked in the head, but she's smart enough to know a swindler when she sees one.'

With this parting shot, the maid shut the door behind her with a bang that made the plaster walls quiver.

Pattern sighed, just once, as she drank her cold tea and ate her stale bread. (The spilling of the tea had done little to soften it.) Her reflection in the glass above the washstand did not hearten her. She was wearing her best black satin dress, a present given to her by the Baroness, but the picture she made in it was not convincing. She looked like a little girl who has got at the costume box.

Pattern straightened her shoulders. She already had the skills to be a good servant. With experience, she would become one of the best. She was not equipped for friendship any more than she was for adventure. Her talents lay elsewhere and she should be proud of that.

And she would not listen to the voice in her head that asked: *What, after all, is the point? Is a good servant of any more value than a reliable clock; of any more worth than a comfortable shoe?*

It was time to make ready her mistress's chamber. Alas, without Mrs Parry to guide her, she was soon lost in the maze of narrow passages and winding stairs designed to keep servants out of sight on their rounds. Expecting to come out in the hallway outside the Grand Duchess's apartments, she found herself instead in a long gallery lined with marble busts of Dukes and Duchesses past. A couple of footmen were idling by the stairs.

One of them, a pimply fellow with a sneer, had seen her hesitate. 'And where are you scurrying off to, Miss Mouse?'

When she explained the matter, he thought it an excellent joke.

'*You?* A lady's maid? Are you even grown enough to tie your own bootlaces?'

'Perhaps it is not a child, but a dwarf,' suggested his friend, who was long-faced with wrinkled stockings.

'I am fully grown in capability, if not in years,' said Pattern, with as much dignity as she could muster. 'And I'm sure I have a good three inches' more height to come.'

The Grand Duchess's apartments, when she finally found them, were in sad disarray. Petticoats and shawls and shoes were strewn on every available surface. There were soapy puddles on the floor and crumbs of cake in the bedclothes. Who had drawn the Grand Duchess's bath and brought her breakfast and helped her dress? If the chambermaids had been at work, there was no sign of it.

Pattern began by throwing open the windows. Then she pulled back the heavy satin drapes around the bed and set about airing the linens. She plumped cushions and straightened furniture. She tidied away the scattered garments to the dressing room, cleaned the smudged looking-glasses and put fresh water in the jugs. In a

backstairs cupboard she
found a broom and cloths
to sweep the room of dust.
After this she washed the
hair combs, replaced the
caps on bottles of lavender
water and almond oil, and
tidied drawers stuffed with
ribbons and pins and other
trinkets. She felt better
now she had work to do.
A neat room always gave
satisfaction to a tidy mind.

Once the chamber was
set to rights, she decided
to take a pile of mending
down to the servants' hall.
It was likely royalty threw
out their clothes as soon
as they were soiled or torn,

but she would not want to presume on it. And in the hall she might find someone who would take pity on her long enough to explain her duties in full.

After the reception she had had so far, she half expected the entire room to fall silent on her entrance, and stare at her with pursed mouths. It was a relief, then, when nobody seemed to notice her slip in. Though perhaps this was small wonder, for her fellows were far too busy with their own affairs – flirting, squabbling, grumbling, gossiping – to pay any mind to hers. She set to quietly darning stockings in a corner, and though a few people glanced her way, it appeared her invisibility trick had been restored.

The noon-time meal, when it was as served, was as plain and badly cooked as her supper the previous night, and eaten amid much elbowing and complaint. From the chatter around her, Pattern gathered there was a great rivalry between Mrs Parry, the Housekeeper, and Mrs Fischer, the Cook, who could only be united in their hatred of Mr Jenkins, the Master of the Household. Perhaps this explained why there was no upper servant present to supervise the conduct of the hall.

Even in less rowdy surroundings, Pattern would have struggled to follow the conversation. The Elffish accent combined a Welsh lilt with gruff Germanic tones, and it took Pattern some while to accustom herself to it. She was forced to say 'I beg your pardon?' three times to an old woman she passed on her way back upstairs.

'She asked if you had seen the keys to the walnut chiffonier,' said the red-headed maid who had brought her breakfast. 'But it seems you are deaf, as well as bungling.'

The girl whisked past someone else Pattern recognized – the pimply footman from the gallery. He gave her a complacent smile.

'Poor Miss Mouse, still scuttling about from one hole to the other! Why do you bother to toil down here? Nobody wants you below stairs, nobody will miss you above.'

Pattern did not deign to answer. Yet she was, in truth, of little use to anyone until her mistress returned.

Perhaps she should use the rest of the day to take a tour of the town and so acquaint herself with her surroundings.

There and then she decided to steal her first ever holiday.

Chapter Four

It will only render you an unprofitable servant if you set your mind on holiday-making, and look upon your duty as drudgery . . . Fun is a thing that does not always lead to the best consequences; and it is possible to be very happy and cheerful without it.

J. Bulcock, *The Duties of a Lady's Maid*

An hour or two on Sundays was the most free time granted at Mrs Minchin's Academy, and to take a whole afternoon for herself was an unimagined liberty. Pattern did not know whether to be

impressed or appalled by her daring.

She made her escape on a footpath that ran parallel to the grand avenue through the wood. It was a walk of two miles, but the further she got from the castle the lighter her step became.

The path emerged a short distance away from the avenue's gatehouse. There Pattern found another gate in the iron railings that enclosed the park, though unlike the ornate main entrance, it was small and rusting – and locked. Pattern took out the set of keys she had found in her bedroom desk, and was gratified to find one that fitted. Leaving the pine wood, she crossed a wide meadow and then a bridge, whereupon she found herself only a little way from the centre of town.

For a capital city, Elffinheim was exceedingly small. Yet Pattern, who had seen many of London's dingy backstreets and few of its famous monuments, was quite ready to be impressed. She wandered through narrow streets of high overhanging houses, across sunny cobbled squares, and along the banks of a shallow brown river lined with lime trees. She admired the little

Gothic cathedral and the parliament building with its high domed roof, and spent a pleasant half-hour in the market, where women sat chattering by their stalls of Welsh cakes and pickled cabbage, smoked sausage and *bara brith*.

One of the stalls sold curious lockets that were open to display bits of feather, coloured beads and what looked like splinters of bone. Pattern bent to look closer. She thought they might be religious relics of some kind.

'A charm to keep you safe, my love,' croaked the aged stallholder. 'No sorcery can get past it, nor monster neither.'

'Sorcery?' Pattern repeated, bewildered.

'Not with one of these beauties around your neck. Cast-iron protection against demons and shape-shifters, and all manner of magical muck! Come, my little dear, I can do you a special price . . .'

But Pattern had already turned away, anxious to lose herself in the crowd. Quaint local customs were all very well, but it seemed Elffinberg harboured some more unsavoury superstitions. Or perhaps the populace was unduly influenced by those romances which Mrs Minchin so despised – the ones full of dangerous ideas and fantastical happenings.

From the general chatter, Pattern heard that the Grand Duchess rarely showed herself to the people, and thus had a reputation for being very proud. Her Uncle Leopold was more popular, but the 'Old Duke', the Grand Duchess's late father, was more beloved than both of them, and widely regarded as a saint. In addition to this, she learned that the price of sugar was criminally high, and that the fishmonger on Denbigh Street was suspected of improper relations with the Captain of the Guard's wife.

This last piece of information was vigorously debated by two women standing in line ahead of her in the cathedral, where she was waiting to view Prince Elffin

Pendraig's shrine. 'But did you hear,' said the elder, 'about the little girl down at the mill?'

Her companion sucked in her cheeks, and looked grave. 'A tragic business,' she agreed. 'Particularly if the rumours are to be believed. The ground round about was scorched black.'

'Yes,' said the other. 'They say all they found of her was . . .' And here she glanced at Pattern, and lowered her voice.

Pattern's curiosity was piqued, but it was, after all, none of her concern. She should only be interested in information that would be of help in waiting on the Grand Duchess. And so as well as seeing the sights, she took care to seek out the most respectable-looking milliner's, draper's and stationer's, and make a note of their address.

Next to the milliner's and its window full of bonnets was a pastry-cook's, with an even more tempting window full of cakes. Pattern could not take her eyes off them. As well as the present of the black satin dress, the kindly Baroness had also given her a small advance on

her wages. Fingering the unfamiliar coins – the Grand Duchess's profile on one side, a dragon on the other – Pattern felt a surge of recklessness. She had already stolen a holiday. Spending wages she hadn't yet earned was a small crime in comparison.

Before she could think better of it, she went into the shop and purchased a square of gingerbread and a glass of lemonade. The dark spices, and the tang of lemons, were the savour of freedom. She had never tasted anything so rich or sweet. Behind the counter, a sign advertised for the position of kitchen assistant. Pattern's head filled with visions of herself in a baker's hat and apron, surrounded by intricate confections of spun sugar and whipped cream . . .

She sighed. The gingerbread was nearly finished, and so was her holiday. She was not a pastry-cook but a lady's maid, and thus far not a very successful one. She must get back before she was missed.

So she brushed the crumbs off her skirts and set off to the castle. But at some point she must have taken a wrong turn, for after rounding several corners, she found herself in a quiet lane that followed the river out of town in the opposite direction to the one she wanted. A row of cottages faced the water, with chickens and children running about, and women taking in washing. A young farmer walking up from the fields completed the peaceful scene.

Pattern was just turning round to retrace her steps when an anguished scream ripped the air.

One of the women had collapsed on the ground. She was clutching a child's shoe to her breast. The farmer was standing to one side, twisting his cap in his hands, his head bowed.

The woman's companions hurried to her side. More people came out of neighbouring houses, forming a fearful huddle at the top of the lane. 'What is it? What's happened?' Pattern asked.

An old lady answered. 'It's her little boy . . . He went missing, out in the hills. And now it looks as if they've found . . . as if all that is left . . . ' She shook her head, unable to go on.

'How terrible! Are there wild animals in these parts?'

A man turned to stare at her. 'And where might you be from, miss?'

Pattern supposed her accent must have given her away. 'I am newly come from England.'

He frowned, and the others in the crowd drew back. 'Then you'd best go back there, quick as you can,' he said. 'These are matters no stranger could hope to understand. Leave Elffish troubles to Elffish folk.'

As Pattern reached the top of the lane, the bereaved mother cried out again, and Pattern saw that shoe she was clutching was blackened and charred, leaving a sooty smear upon her apron. She was glad to leave a scene of such grief, yet she could not get it out of her head. She was wondering, too, about the conversation she had overheard in the cathedral, about the little girl from the mill.

The gingerbread lay heavy in her belly; the lemonade had left a sour taste in her mouth. As she crossed the bridge out of Elffinheim and saw the castle's rooftops rise above the trees, she was sure she had been found out, and would have Mrs Parry to answer to. The golden afternoon light was fading, and the wood looked very black.

She struggled to fit the key in the gate.

'Allow me, miss.'

A man had come up behind her and taken the key. He was tall, and almost entirely in shadow. Her heart jumped in her chest. Then, bowing his head a little, the gentleman pushed open the gate and she saw he

was dressed in the fine dark cloth that marked him as an upper servant. He was an altogether elegant figure: wintry-blond and aquiline, and scented faintly with aniseed.

'Pardon me,' he said, 'but I don't believe I have had the pleasure of your acquaintance. May I ask the nature of your business at the castle?'

With a sinking heart, Pattern explained her situation; yet the gentleman smiled. 'Then you are most welcome. I hope you find everything to your liking, and that you will be content in your work.'

She was so surprised she could only stammer her thanks.

'Allow me to introduce myself. My name is Mr Madoc and I am valet to His Royal Highness Prince Leopold.'

The Prince's valet! Pattern eyed him with new interest and respect. He, too, seemed young for his position, for in spite of his stately air, he looked to be still in his twenties. Her respect only increased as they walked together through the wood, for Madoc answered all her questions very civilly, and was generous with his advice. In return, he asked a deal of questions about herself, and what she thought of Elffinberg thus far.

'You should be careful,' he told her, 'walking alone out here when the light is fading.'

'Yes, I heard in town that the countryside has it dangers.'

'Oh, indeed?'

'There was talk – that some little children had been taken. I thought it must be wild animals, but . . .' She faltered, for Madoc had come to a halt, and was staring at her with a strange intensity. 'Well, I am sure such rumours spring up everywhere, and become exaggerated in the telling.'

They began to walk on, and his sigh was like the whisper of the pines. 'Elffinberg is so small and so quiet, much of the world has forgotten about us. Yet you may find that we are not quite as sleepy as we appear.' His eyes gleamed in the shadows. 'We have our secrets, and our burdens too. Pray that you do not have to share them.'

Chapter Five

ംരാ ംരാ

Suppose that you are once in a place; it must be a very bad one indeed if you cannot make it good with a little management.

J. Bulcock, *The Duties of a Lady's Maid*

ംരാ ംരാ

Pattern's second day in Royal Servitude began in much the same way as the first: the red-headed housemaid – Dilys – was just as unfriendly, the breakfast bread just as dry. She was informed the Grand Duchess had returned from visiting her godmama in the early hours of the morning, and was now resting. Pattern had nothing to do but sharpen her sewing needles and rehearse her curtsy.

At eleven o'clock she was summoned to the Royal Presence.

Grand folding doors swung open before her, under the guidance of two impish page-boys. The sitting room of the Grand Duchess's suite was an enormous apartment, barren and colourless, except for a tapestry over the fireplace that depicted a hunting scene in faded tones of scarlet and green. There was a chessboard floor of black and white marble, a few severely straight-backed chairs, and a shining oak table. None of this seemed designed for either comfort or ornamentation.

Lounging on an angular daybed before the empty fire, and swinging her feet, was the Grand Duchess.

'Oh,' she said. 'It's you.'

Pattern waited, head bowed and hands clasped.

The silence stretched on. 'So,' said the Grand Duchess at last, 'my godmama says I am to give you a chance. She says you are not a spy, but a poor orphan.'

'Yes, Your Highness.'

'I am an orphan too, you know.'

'Yes, Your Highness. I am very sorry.'

'Do you mean you are sorry for you, or for me?'

'I am sorry for anyone who is left alone in the world.'

'For it is a wicked world, is it not?'

Pattern thought. 'Yes,' she said. 'It certainly can be.'

'The Baroness von Bliven does not agree. I have powerful enemies – many persons who conspire against me. Yet the Baroness refuses to believe it. She treats me like a nonsensical child. She is a good woman, but a stupid one. Who . . .' The cold little voice caught for a moment. 'Well. For all that, she was my last friend in this whole miserable country. And now she is dying, perhaps already dead.'

Pattern finally dared raise her eyes. The Grand Duchess's were red-rimmed. Her black hair straggled limply about her shoulders. She was dressed in a gown of canary-coloured silk, with the buttons done up crooked. It was not a colour that suited her.

Her face was pointed of chin, and wide of brow. Her muddy green eyes looked too big for it, an effect exaggerated by the shadows around them. She was altogether too pinched and sallow. Yet when she looked at Pattern, her gaze did not waver, and her expression was as haughty as her voice.

'So I suppose I have little choice but to see what you are made of.'

The Grand Duchess swung herself off the daybed and went to the windows. They looked across a vast terrace and vast lawn. Distant vistas showed lakes and summer houses at the end of avenues that converged on a woodland. Beyond them rose the misted grey and purple of the mountains.

'What do you think of my castle?'

'It is exceedingly grand, Your Highness.'

'It is an exceedingly grand prison. My courtiers are my gaolers, my servants are spies. I should be pitied, not envied for it.'

Pattern thought of the ten-year-old scullery maid she had passed in the kitchen that morning, whose hands were red and raw, and whose skinny back was curved from sixteen-hour days hunched over crusted pans and dirty floors. She thought of the orphanage in which she had spent her early years: the damp walls and draughty windows, the sour-faced matron with her swishing cane. She thought of the woman by the river yesterday, weeping for her lost child.

But: 'Yes, Your Highness,' was all she said.

In truth, Pattern's first impressions of the castle proved correct. It was neither properly furnished nor lighted nor kept in order. Perhaps this was hardly surprising, given the scale of the place, with its corridors as wide as streets and rooms the size of churches. It was not so much like a prison, she thought, as a very splendid mausoleum.

By the end of her first week, she had begun to settle into a routine. At seven o'clock she was woken by Dilys with her breakfast and washing water. At eight she woke the Grand Duchess (no easy task, and accompanied by much complaint and hiding under the bedcovers). She brought her mistress her tea, and any correspondence. Then she ran her bath, helped her dress, tidied her room and did her hair.

Prayers were gabbled through in the servants' hall at a quarter past nine, while her mistress took her breakfast. The Grand Duchess had lessons most mornings, with 'accomplishments' – dancing, drawing, music – in the afternoon. Pattern was much more interested in the morning programme. Sitting quietly in a corner, waiting to be useful, she took in as much as she was able. The Grand Duchess's tutors were all elderly and dry, but Pattern thought – even if the Grand Duchess did not – that nothing in the world could make history dull or geography colourless. Even Latin verse had its charms.

Otherwise, it was a life of unvaried and empty ceremony. Much of it was spent accompanying the Grand Duchess on social calls, in which ladies of the court exchanged meaningless pleasantries in stuffy rooms with too much furniture. In the evening, escorted by the Chamberlain, the Grand Duchess would lead a procession of dusty courtiers to dinner. Afterwards, she would take a cup of cocoa and play solitaire alone in her room. She did not have, nor appeared to want, any friends of her own age. She had a dread of being seen by the populace, and on the rare occasions they left the castle, the State Coach's windows were always closed. For the Baroness von Bliven's funeral, the Grand Duchess kept her face entirely veiled.

There was no less intrigue below stairs, and despite the disorder, the hierarchy was just as rigid. Yet although the servants were ill-managed, at least there was liveliness and bustle among them. Apart from morning prayers and her meals – dinner at midday, tea at four, supper at half past nine – Pattern was with the Grand Duchess most of the day.

She did her best to be useful. She was sure to always have fresh flowers in the bedchamber. She re-sewed fallen hems, and re-attached loose buttons. She mixed a rose-water cold cream for the Grand Duchess's complexion, and a herbal draught to help her sleep. She consulted Parisian fashion plates to keep abreast of the latest modes in hair and dress. Yet despite her best efforts, her mistress showed little interest in her toilette, and her clothes continued to attract all manner of stains and tears. Her nightgowns and slippers suffered the most, and Pattern often wondered what happened to them in the midnight hour after she had departed for her own bed.

However, the Grand Duchess's carelessness with her dress proved Pattern's saving grace with Dilys. Pattern made the housemaid a present of an emerald-green fur-trimmed pelisse that had been got at by moths, and which the Grand Duchess had told her to dispose of. It was a lady's maid's privilege to make use of cast-offs however she wished, and Pattern reasoned that the emerald was much better suited to Dilys's colouring.

This was something with which Dilys heartily agreed. Thereafter, although the maid was no more friendly, at least the water in Pattern's wash-jug was warm, and her tea was mostly hot.

Pattern rarely saw Madoc in the servants' hall. In spite of his height, he had the same facility for disappearing into the background as she. But on the rare occasions when they did encounter each other, he was always sure to smile and bid her good day.

She continued to puzzle over what she witnessed on her first visit into the city, and the valet's remarks about secrets and burdens. Sometimes she would come upon people whispering in dark corners and stairwells, and when they saw her they would fall silent, their eyes watchful and cold. Pattern knew she was a stranger, and a foreign one at that. She told herself it was most likely the whispers meant nothing at all.

But if these people were exchanging mere tittle-tattle, then why did they look so afraid?

Chapter Six

Consider what a few pounds or shillings will avail you, if you lose your character.

J. Bulcock, *The Duties of a Lady's Maid*

The following day Pattern had occasion to pass through the Mirror Gallery, a coldly glittering cavern in which the court gathered to play cards. She was looking for a fan the Grand Duchess had dropped. She caught the scent of aniseed, and suddenly there was Madoc, who seemed to have shimmered out of the glass itself, holding the missing fan in his hand.

'A very good morning to you, Miss Pattern. Would now be an opportune moment to speak to my master, Prince Leopold? He wishes to have a word.'

It *was* an opportune moment, for her mistress had retired to her bed with a headache and did not wish to be disturbed. Pattern was nonetheless a little apprehensive at the summoning. This would be her first encounter with the Grand Duchess's uncle and guardian, for until now the Prince had been holidaying at his hunting lodge.

'Come now,' said Madoc, when he saw her hesitate. 'I promise you the man won't bite. At least, not as hard or hungrily as some.'

This time, there was something a little malicious in his smile.

'Thank you, but even if he did, no doubt I would survive to tell the tale.'

Madoc was amused. 'So a fighting spirit lurks beneath that timid exterior! My apologies if I have underestimated you, Miss Pattern.' He looked at her again. 'Hmm ... But I begin to suspect I am not the only one. Could it be that our little mouse is considerably less tame than she appears?'

Pattern was not used to this kind of scrutiny. There was a sharpness to Madoc's gaze that she found unsettling. So she ducked her head and followed after him in her mousiest manner.

She had to admit that she was curious to meet the Prince. The commoners spoke of him as a model of generosity and courtly charm, yet according to the Grand Duchess, he was a criminal mastermind who wanted to steal her throne and turn her subjects against her before she came of age and could take her place on the Council of State.

'But why then,' Pattern had ventured, 'don't you show yourself to the people more? Surely if they knew you better, Your Highness, their loyalty would greatly increase?'

'You think I should gad about, cutting ribbons and christening ships? Embracing babies?'

'Well . . .'

'My subjects will never love me for who I am,' the

Grand Duchess had said sourly. 'I am their insurance, that's all. Their sacrificial lamb. And if the time comes, they will offer me up on the altar without shedding a tear. They know it, and I know it. So I don't see why I should grovel after their good opinion.'

What sacrifice, and on what altar? But the Grand Duchess would not be drawn on the matter.

Pattern thought back to this conversation as she followed Madoc to her meeting with his master. Prince Leopold had nearly a whole wing of the castle to himself, and the interview took place in his study. The man himself was seated at his desk, and bounced up when she entered, smiling and twinkling.

'Good Lord! You're even smaller than they said!' He laughed heartily. 'It seems to me that servants' halls in England must resemble nurseries – with infant cooks, pint-sized butlers, and valets who are mere babes-in-arms. Ha, ha!'

Pattern did not know how to respond to this, but the Prince seemed content to enjoy his own joke. He was small and plump, with round, rosy cheeks like those of a

child. His gold curls were thinning, and the skin around his merry blue eyes was lined, giving him the appearance of an ageing yet sprightly cherub.

There was something a little whimsical, too, about the furnishing of his study. Every available surface was cluttered with china ornaments. Miniature teapots and decorative jugs rubbed against flocks of shepherdesses and harlequins, cupids and gypsies, and ballerinas with billowing skirts.

'Charming, aren't they?' the Prince said, though Pattern had not remarked on them. 'Porcelain has always been a passion of mine. Indeed, I flatter myself that I am something of a connoisseur.'

'It is a very handsome collection, Your Highness,' said Pattern, whose first thought was pity for whoever was tasked with the dusting.

'I am glad you think so. Very glad! One is never too young to cultivate an artistic sensibility.'

Her eye was drawn to a particularly large and ornate urn, which had fearsome dragons as the handles, and was painted with a forest of exotic blooms.

The Prince saw her looking and positively preened. 'A gift from a Chinese dignitary, and close associate of mine. China was the birthplace of porcelain, you know. But I truly believe that our Elffish potters have surpassed theirs and are now the finest in the world.' He picked up a simpering flower-girl, inspected its base, then set it back in place with a tender pat to its head. 'Now then! I did not call you here to chatter about ceramics, agreeable as that would be. I wished to enquire as to how you are settling in.'

A prince of the realm, enquiring as to the well-being of a lady's maid? Pattern resisted the impulse to raise an eyebrow.

'I am quite comfortable, thank you, Your Highness.'

'Truly? My niece has a reputation for being somewhat contrary, to say the least. Still, I trust you will look after her well. The Grand Duchess Arianwen's welfare is my first concern. First and best!' He looked at her keenly. 'But perhaps she has told you otherwise?'

'The Grand Duchess does not confide in me, Your Highness.'

'She does not trust you, then.'

'She is very . . . cautious, Your Highness.'

'Paranoid, you mean. Oh, there's no use denying it.' The Prince sighed heavily, and shook his head. 'Perhaps she is having a quiet spell. Perhaps! But you need to prepare yourself. Yes, I'm afraid there will be all manner of rantings and ravings. All kinds of wild talk.' He drew nearer. 'You will tell me, won't you? If she mistreats you, if she gives way to these violent passions? I can be a useful friend to you, child. An attentive and liberal patron. You have only to keep me informed of your mistress's state of mind. If you were able to gain her trust, that would be even better. I am only concerned for her health.'

He was pressing a heavy coin into her hand.

'There now! A little something to welcome you to

court. It's only right for young people to treat themselves from time to time.' The Prince moved back, smiling widely. 'Ours is a glorious country, Pattern. A land of opportunity. Yes, there are many opportunities for good girls who mind their tongues, and know which side their bread is buttered on.'

He tapped the side of his nose and winked at her. 'Ha! Ha, ha!'

The Grand Duchess's headache continued until very late. She soon tired of being left on her own, and so Pattern spent the rest of the day running back and forth fetching smelling salts, fruit cordials and fashion papers, in between fanning the Royal Cheeks and holding ice to the Royal Forehead. By midnight, she was ready to drop with exhaustion, whereas the Grand Duchess declared herself much recovered, and far too restless for bed. Instead, she wished to browse the library. 'And you must come with me, Pattern, to hold the lamp and carry the books, and in case there is anything I think I might want.'

Pattern liked the library. To wander through it was like being in a pleasant maze, whose walls and towers were formed of gilt-edged books. However, it was over a mile-long walk to get there, and her legs were already very weary. They had just turned into the hallway leading to its doors when they saw Madoc emerge from the library with a pile of books and glide away in the opposite direction.

'Ugh! That horrid man!' whispered the Grand Duchess with a shudder. 'Always lurking and smirking! I think I should hate him even if he did not serve my uncle.'

'Mr Madoc took me to meet with Prince Leopold this morning, Your Highness.'

Pattern was not quite sure how she had come to make the confession. It certainly had a dramatic effect upon the Grand Duchess, who came to an immediate halt. Although the hallway was dark and deserted, she drew Pattern into an alcove and glanced about her before she spoke.

'M-my uncle?'

'Yes, Your Highness.'

She breathed in sharply. 'What did you make of him?'

It was a good question, and one that led to another: whose confidence should she keep? Looking at her mistress, Pattern was not entirely sure of the truth of the headache, but she was certain that the girl was not well. There were always dark circles under her eyes, and her hands often trembled. Pattern doubted she slept more than a couple of hours each night.

Perhaps Prince Leopold was right, and the balance of the Grand Duchess's mind was disturbed. Yet Pattern had promised the Baroness von Bliven that she would serve her mistress faithfully, and a promise to a dying woman is even more binding than the ordinary kind.

She had not forgotten the Baroness's advice to *trust no one*. However, trust was a risk Pattern had to take. So would the Grand Duchess.

'The Prince was entirely affable, Your Highness,' Pattern answered, after only a short pause. 'And he promised that his kindness to me would only increase.

For he gave me money and asked me to gain your confidence, so that I could keep him informed as to the state of your health.' She reached into her pocket, pulled out the Prince's coin, and gave it to the Grand Duchess. 'I would rather not have money I didn't earn by honest means.'

'So your loyalty is not for sale?' the Grand Duchess replied. Her tone was doubtful. 'Why? I have shown you no particular favour.'

'Favoured or not, your health is your own business, just the same as your dreams or fears or any other private thing. It is not the Prince's place to pry into such matters. Nor mine.'

'Ah, you would not wish to know my dreams, Pattern. They are full of terrors. As for my fears, I have so many that the weight of them quite exhausts me. But whatever my uncle would like you to think, I am not mad.' She looked at her searchingly. 'I hope you believe me. Because . . . because I would like very much to believe *you*. Even if I'm not able to just yet.'

CHAPTER SEVEN

❧ ❦

Fidelity, indeed, is that which is more respected in a servant than any other quality, and sooner or later you will meet with your reward, if you approve yourself faithful and worthy to be trusted.

J. Bulcock, *The Duties of a Lady's Maid*

❧ ❦

Over the next week, Pattern felt increasingly able to disregard Prince Leopold's warnings about his niece's mental health. She had yet to witness any rantings and ravings. In fact, the Grand Duchess made new efforts to say please and thank you, and even ordered the kitchens to make up crumpets and anchovy paste, two delicacies that she believed people from England had a particular passion for. 'I should not like you to get homesick, Pattern,' she said, before rather spoiling the effect by adding, 'I can't abide people who mope about the place. Low spirits in others is a frightful bore.'

The Grand Duchess's own spirits had somewhat improved, and there was less talk of the mysterious threats that beset her. Her only demonstrably peculiar behaviour was a habit of talking in her sleep. The first time Pattern witnessed this, she had come to wake her mistress for breakfast, and heard murmurs and laughter from within the chamber. Once through the door, Pattern looked around the otherwise empty room in surprise.

'What are you gawking at?' the Grand Duchess asked through her yawns.

'I beg your pardon, Your Highness. I thought you had a visitor.'

'*That* is not very likely. I am not in the habit of entertaining guests in my nightgown.'

'I am sorry, Your Highness, but I heard voices. That is, I heard your voice.'

The Grand Duchess looked momentarily confused, though she recovered quickly. 'I was saying my morning prayers, Pattern. As I hope you do too – for my continued good health, and the safety of the land.'

Pattern was not entirely convinced of this, but let it pass. Then, the following night, as she was making ready for bed, she realized she had left a shawl in need of mending in the Grand Duchess's room. Her mistress had asked her to take particular care of it, since it had belonged to her mama, and so Pattern resolved to retrieve it before the morning.

Pausing outside the door, she heard murmurs from within, but concluded it must be her mistress talking in her sleep. She crept in quietly, expecting to be in and out in less than a minute, and was quite taken aback to find the Grand Duchess sitting bolt upright in bed. However, the girl appeared to still be asleep. Her eyes were closed, and her hair was tumbling undone about her shoulders, as she swayed back and forth, as if in a trance.

'I am free of you,' she was muttering, in a pleading kind of sing-song. 'You cannot reach me. Your time is over, done. I am free of you. You cannot reach me. Your time is over . . .'

Suddenly the Grand Duchess gave a hoarse chuckle. Her eyes opened and through some trick of light in the shadowy room, they appeared all black, with no whites showing at all. Her voice became a rasp.

'I see you, Princess. I know your scent. I can hear the throb of your heart, the tick of fear through your veins. My time is not over. It draws closer by the day.'

Dreams are mysterious things, and talking in one's sleep is common enough. Jane at Mrs Minchin's Academy had often woken the girls at night by babbling all kinds of nonsense about pots and pans and jam for tea. All the same, Pattern felt an icy breath on her neck. Then the Grand Duchess turned her head and fixed Pattern in her strange blank gaze.

'Little girl. Stranger from a strange land. I see you too. You are watching and waiting, and so am I. You are not afraid yet, but you will be. *You will be.*'

This last was a low, lingering hiss.

Suddenly, the room's shadows seemed alive with malice. It brushed against Pattern's skin and whispered in her skull, and for a moment she felt this was *her* nightmare, not the Grand Duchess's. She had to give herself a good hard pinch to get over it. Then she went to the bed and shook her mistress into wakefulness.

The Grand Duchess came to with a jolt, and peered at Pattern with bleary annoyance. 'Whatever are you doing here? It is surely not time for breakfast.'

'No, Your Highness.' Pattern did her best to hide

her disquiet, and explained about the shawl and the sleep-talking as matter-of-factly as she was able. 'You seemed somewhat . . . agitated. I thought you might be unwell.' Her eye was caught by the Grand Duchess's bedroom slippers, which lay torn and muddied on the floor. They would have to be thrown out – the second pair this week. 'Forgive me: is it possible you walk in your sleep too?'

'Don't be absurd! Sometimes, when I cannot sleep, and am bored of counting sheep, I take a turn about the grounds, that's all. I find the fresh night air settles me. As for the sleep-talking – didn't you tell me my dreams were my own affair?

'I did, Your Highness.'

'Then kindly speak no more of it.'

But the next occurrence proved more troublesome, since it took place in public. It was not unknown for the Grand Duchess to drift off during lengthy social engagements, partly due to the tedium of such gatherings and partly because she slept so poorly at night. On this occasion – a ladies' tea party in

aid of the Society for the Beautification of Historic Monuments – she had contrived to position her chair partway behind a folding screen so that she could doze in peace. Pattern, sitting close by, was charged with nudging her awake if her participation was required.

Tea had been served and the strudel was mostly in crumbs when a low chuckle came from behind the Grand Duchess's screen. She mumbled something urgent yet indistinguishable that nonetheless caused those nearby to turn and stop their chatter. Then, even as Pattern shook her arm, her voice began to huskily declaim:

'I thirst for blue air, and freedom, and the hot tang of blood . . .'

The whole room was listening now. Pattern poked her mistress in the ribs, but to no avail.

'When I am called,' she continued, still so low and deep, 'I will answer. And then I will rise. I may be summoned, but I am never ruled. I shall not be mastered, I cannot be tamed—'

Pattern poked her again, harder. The Grand Duchess's eyes opened but there seemed little life in them. Something must be done.

'Remarkable, Your Highness,' said Pattern, clapping her hands with all the enthusiasm she could muster, though in truth she was most disturbed. 'What an accomplished performance!' She turned to face the assembled guests. 'There is a new play in London that is all the rage, and so I have been teaching Her Highness the most admired speeches. She has just favoured us with an extract.'

'And what is the name of this fashionable drama?' enquired a double-chinned dowager.

'It is *The*... um ... *Butler's Revenge*, my lady,' Pattern improvised. 'The previously untold story of . . . er . . . Cleopatra's manservant.' She was glad to see the Grand Duchess looking more like her usual self, and hoped she had the wit to follow Pattern's lead. 'So you see it is a historical piece, and thus very educational.'

'Educational,' the Grand Duchess repeated blearily, but in her normal voice. 'Exactly so.'

The assembled ladies followed Pattern's example and gave dutiful applause.

When they were alone again, the Grand Duchess was full of thanks. 'That was very quick thinking, Pattern. Very quick! Even so, I hope wild tales of the incident do not find their way to my uncle.'

Pattern feared it was already too late. Several of the ladies had clapped most doubtfully, and there had been much shaking of heads and sucking of teeth on their departure. Furthermore, on her next visit to the servants' hall, Madoc had glided past, observing, 'You are full of surprises, Miss Pattern. Not only a lady's maid, but a theatrical agent! I hope you do not intend to turn our Duchess into a pantomime dame.' Pattern did not want to make her mistress more agitated than she already was, however.

Rather than fretting about the peculiar nature of her outburst, the Grand Duchess's energies were fixated on what Prince Leopold would make of it.

'He warned you, a mere servant girl, that I was a lunatic. Imagine what he must say to people who actually *matter*,' she complained. 'The villain wants to spread lies that I am unfit to rule, so he can lock me up in a madhouse and throw away the key. Yes, I can see every crooked twist of his mind . . .' She frowned. 'But Pattern, I never know what you are thinking. Your face is as blank as a bowl of milk.'

Observations such as this surprised Pattern. It seemed a miracle that the clamorous whirl inside her head was undetectable to others. However, she was always glad to find this was the case. 'That is because my thoughts are my own, Your Highness, and I need to keep them that way. I have little else, after all.'

'Yet you don't sound the least bit pitiful about it. Lord! You must think me prodigiously spoilt.'

'I think you are unhappy, Your Highness.'

'Are *you* unhappy, Pattern?'

'Often, Your Highness.'

As soon as she said it, she wished the impudent words back in her mouth. It was not a question she had ever imagined having to answer – she had not even consciously asked it of herself. Yet the Grand Duchess

did not seem offended by her frankness. She merely nodded.

'It is because you are alone. It is a cruel thing, I know. Perhaps you have always been alone, but I have not, so I understand the difference. My mama died when I was born, and then my darling papa died ten years later. His closest friends, who would also have been mine, and served my interests, have all been exiled or imprisoned. Now even my godmama the Baroness is gone.' She sighed. 'You see, it is my former happiness that makes my current situation so hard to bear.'

'I am sorry, Your Highness. Truly.'

'Then . . .' The Grand Duchess twisted her hands, suddenly shy. 'Perhaps . . . perhaps I shall try and trust you, after all? As you are so clever, and we are both unhappy and alone? What do you think?'

At that, Pattern looked her in the eye, more boldly than she had looked at anyone in her life. Her heart trembled.

'I think that I would like that very much.'

CHAPTER EIGHT

The books you ought to read, next to those which are calculated to inspire you with pious reflections, are such as may give you instruction in the practical duties of your situation.

J. Bulcock, *The Duties of a Lady's Maid*

In spite of their newfound intimacy, Pattern saw little of the Grand Duchess over the next two days. It was close to the anniversary of her coronation, and a state banquet was to mark the occasion. One hundred and fifty guests were expected, many of whom came to

the court early to pay their respects, and the Grand Duchess's time was almost entirely taken up by these visitors.

Pattern was glad not to be directly involved with the preparations. It had taken three days just to lay the banqueting table. Under the supervision of the Warden of the Silver Vault and the Curator of the Glass and China Pantry, two thousand pieces of cutlery had to be properly distributed, and six glasses laid out for each guest. A senior steward was responsible for personally folding one hundred and fifty napkins into the shape of daffodils.

The Grand Duchess sent for Pattern the night before the banquet. Pattern had begun to wonder if her mistress had second thoughts about confiding in her, and was surprised by how anxious and unhappy the idea made her feel. She realized how much she would like to trust the Grand Duchess in turn. Being needed was one thing; being *wanted* was another, and was something Pattern had little experience of. And what if the girl had changed her mind? However, as soon as Pattern came into the room all such doubts were set aside, for the Grand Duchess seized her hands and, even though there was nobody else to hear them, whispered hotly in her ear.

'Thank heavens we are alone at last! I have been thinking what to do all day – what I may speak of, and how much must stay silent. I am so confused! It is my burden, you see. A secret that no one must ever know. It is for your own sake, Pattern, believe me. And yet . . . yet I am feeling reckless all the same. Come, we are going to the library again!'

Once there, she snatched the oil lamp from Pattern and hastened into the maze of stacks and shelving, examining every corner to check they were alone and unobserved. There was a door concealed in a wall of books that Pattern had never noticed before. She assumed it would take them into one of the rat-runs used by the servants, but instead it led to a stairwell with rough stone walls and crude, uneven steps, whose edges had been worn smooth by the passage of many feet over many years; centuries, perhaps.

'We are now in all that remains of the Old Castle,' the Grand Duchess told her, voice low. 'It has been so completely swallowed up by the new one that most people do not realize that there is any remnant left, or else have forgotten how to reach it. This is part of Prince Elffin's own fortress.'

The ancient stairway led up to a similarly ancient door, very thick and squat, its wood black with age. 'Nobody may enter here but me. I have forbidden it. Besides,' she said, fishing in her pocket, 'I am the only one who has a key.'

The door opened on to a gallery, with a ceiling of vaulted stone, and panelled walls. Traces of faded gilt clung to the carved wood. The Grand Duchess held up the lamp to show the row of portraits lining either wall. They were all of young girls: each and every one richly dressed, and sad-eyed.

'Behold,' the Grand Duchess said. 'The Hall of Maidens.'

'Who are they, Your Highness?'

'They are my ancestors. Royal Princesses of the House of Elffin.'

There were about twenty portraits, spanning a time frame of over five hundred years. As far as Pattern could judge from the style of painting and the subjects' dress, the greater concentration of portraits dated from the late Middle Ages through to the reign of England's Elizabeth I. There were considerably fewer portraits for later years. The most recent painting showed a girl wearing the costume of a hundred years before. She looked not much older than twelve.

'Is there to be a portrait of you, Your Highness?'

It was the wrong question.

The Grand Duchess drew herself up; for a moment Pattern thought she was about to strike her. 'God forbid,' she said, crossing herself. 'God forbid.'

'I – I am very sorry, Your Highness,' Pattern stammered. 'I didn't mean to offend –'

The Grand Duchess drew a shaky breath. 'No, it is me who should be sorry. The offence is not yours. For how could you know that every girl on this wall died young, and that these paintings are their funeral monument?'

Pattern looked at the painted faces, the quiet mouths and melancholy eyes, and felt a coldness trickle down her back.

'A fine collection, is it not?' This time the Grand Duchess's voice was bitter and black. 'Oh yes, there is much to admire in the House of Elffin, and its saintly dead.'

This conversation with the Grand Duchess disturbed Pattern more than she liked to admit. She could not get the sleep-talking interludes out of her mind either. There was something so ominous about them, something unnatural. She herself did not sleep much for what remained of the night and, rising before dawn, she made haste back to the library. There she consulted several learned tomes on the history of Elffinberg. She was surprised to find them as dull as they were brief, for the Grand Duchy's history appeared to be almost entirely without incident. The country engaged in no wars and suffered no invasions; there had been no struggles for the succession, no civil unrest. An occasional crop failure or outbreak of influenza was as close as the country ever came to crisis.

Only one book diverted from this happy narrative. It was a tattered old thing that Pattern only found by chance, since it had been carelessly shelved between the collected journals of the Royal Elffish Society of Ceramicists and the memoirs of a long-dead Lady of the Bedchamber. The history it recounted was much as she had read before, except for a list of dates at the front of the book. Although these dates chiefly related to the ducal succession, there was a recurring entry

that greatly intrigued her, and referred simply to a 'Great Bane'. The last 'Great Bane' occurred just over a hundred years ago. A 'bane' was a kind of curse, Pattern believed. She thought back to the Hall of Maidens, and wondered if perhaps it referred to the untimely death of Princesses . . .

'So you are a reader too.'

She jumped.

'Mr Madoc, you startled me.'

The valet had emerged from behind a tower of shelving, and was surveying the book in her hand with interest. Though she had done nothing wrong, she somehow felt herself at fault. 'I, er – that is – Her Royal Highness said I could make use of the library.'

'How generous of her.' The valet spoke with an ironical edge. 'Perhaps she is not aware of how dangerous a book can be. An educated mind may think for itself, and so grow restless.'

'I merely wished to know a little of the history of the country.'

'So you are interested in facts? Yes, I can guess the

kind of reader you are – you seek to understand the world through its statistics, and have little patience for tales of magic and adventure.'

Pattern resented his condescending tone. 'Is that what you prefer to read?'

'Those of us who are alone in the world, and must survive on our wits and our toil, rarely have the luxury of reading for pleasure.' Madoc ran his finger down a crumbling spine. 'But don't give up on the fairy tales entirely, Miss Pattern. The old stories are often more true than one thinks.'

Madoc's sudden appearances made her uncomfortable. So did his way of looking as if he was enjoying a private joke – and one that was at her expense. She found she did not wish to explain her particular interest in the history of Elffinberg.

Pattern returned to her room, deep in thought, just as Dilys was arriving with her breakfast. Her eye was caught by a locket glinting at the girl's neck. It reminded her of the stall of amulets in the marketplace, the ones that were supposed to protect people from sorcery.

Feeling a little foolish, and fully expecting a sarcastic reply, she asked Dilys if she believed in magic.

'I believe in our Good Lord, and that He will defend the innocent from the snares of wickedness,' Dilys replied virtuously. 'But the devil works in mysterious ways, and so do his demons.'

'How do you mean?'

'I mean I heard of a woman who was bewitched so that whenever she tried to speak, nothing but black slime came out of her mouth. And there was a baby, back in my village, who got stolen by spirits, and replaced with a pile of dead leaves.'

Pattern felt increasingly out of her depth. Still, she pressed on. 'Then do you know what a "Great Bane" might be?'

At this, the housemaid started violently, and almost dropped the tray.

'Good gracious, Miss Pattern, why would you ask?'

'It was . . . something I read.'

'Well, it's a deal of nonsense, I'm sure.' The housemaid unsteadily set down the tray. 'And nothing that need trouble us now, God willing.' She crossed herself, and tugged on the amulet for good measure. Then something of her old snap returned. '*You* should keep your twitchy mouse nose out of it, in any event.'

The door slammed behind her.

After the dark hints and sorrowful looks of the night before, Pattern expected to find the Grand Duchess in very low spirits. In fact, her mistress was exceedingly cheerful, and already up and dressed when Pattern went to wake her. First, she made her a present of a pearl brooch – 'You must wear it always, as a reminder that we are friends.' And then she announced that she wished Pattern to know her better – 'So I will begin with my beginnings, and show you my darling papa and mama.'

She led the way to the Throne Room, where a portrait of the late Grand Duke looked down on his former seat. It had been painted in the year of his death, and perhaps he was already sick, for even allowing for the artist's flattery, his face appeared careworn, and deeply lined. Yet he looked, as Pattern

said, a most dignified and kindly man.

From there they went to the ballroom, with its parquet floor as wide and shining as a lake, and chandeliers that dripped from the ceiling like crystal stalactites. Here it was a painting of the Grand Duchess's mother that dominated the room. She was slim and raven-haired, with sloping white shoulders and laughing eyes.

'I hope I grow up to be as beautiful as my mama. Everyone expects a princess to look the part. It is not enough for us to be kind and clever, but we must be as decorative as the heroine of any fairy tale.' The Grand Duchess sighed. 'And what of *your* parents, Pattern? For I wish to know you better, too.'

Pattern explained that she knew next to nothing about them, and related the story of the disaster at sea.

'Oh well,' said the Grand Duchess carelessly. 'Immigration is always a risky business. If my guard had caught up with them, they would have been put to death in any case. People are not allowed to leave Elffinberg. They have to ask for my permission.

Yes – even my godmama the Baroness.'

Pattern had to sit down abruptly in one of the spindly gold chairs. It felt as if her legs had given way from under her. 'The state *executes* those who attempt to leave it, Your Highness?'

'Well, it's a fearful shame, and I'm very sorry about it, naturally, but we can't have people leaving the country willy-nilly and selling secrets to our enemies.'

Pattern was scarcely able to hide her indignation.

'But, Highness . . . what enemies does Elffinberg have?'

And what secrets?

'We are a tiny country, surrounded by many large and aggressive ones. If it were not for . . .' The Grand Duchess stopped confusedly. 'Well. Never mind. And now you are upset! Oh dear. Perhaps when I am come of age, and have real power at last, I will find another – better – way to stop people leaving.' She looked at Pattern anxiously. 'I am very sorry for your parents. I'm sure they were good people, whoever they were. Come, I've a notion that will cheer you up.'

CHAPTER NINE

What I would particularly caution you against, however, is giving advice when you are not asked, or thrusting your opinion upon your mistress, whether she seems desirous of having it or not.

J. Bulcock, *The Duties of a Lady's Maid*

The Grand Duchess's grand notion was that Pattern should procure for her a maid's uniform, and that thus disguised, she and Pattern should walk into the city together.

'I mean to go about my subjects as a humble servant

girl and hear what they say about me. Like Harry the Fifth of England did, before his battle with the French. It will be the most marvellous fun!'

Pattern thought this was neither wise nor practical, let alone marvellous fun, but the Grand Duchess overrode all her objections. 'Now, you must remember, Pattern, not to call me "Highness". You may call me Eleri, as it is my favourite of my names, and there are plenty of ordinary girls who share it. And because we are to play at being equals, I shall call you by your first name too. Isn't it funny I don't know it?'

'Pattern is the only name I have, Your Highness.'

'*Eleri*, remember. Dear me – you are very slow today! But I don't understand this business of having no Christian name. I have four, and even that is considered mean by royal standards. Did you forget yours or merely lose it?'

'There is no record of what my parents christened me, and the orphanage neglected to fill the gap.'

'Oh, then you can take whatever name you like! I should think that a marvellous liberty. Though you had

better not choose one of mine,' the Grand Duchess added hastily, 'as I do not think that would be quite proper.'

Her own name, there for the choosing! Now she came to think of it, it was odd she had not taken the opportunity to pick one before . . . Yet Pattern's mind was a perfect blank. 'I think I will know the right name when I find it, Your Hi— Eleri. For now, plain Pattern will have to do.'

The escapade began with a visit to the laundry. Since it was not appropriate to clean a bootboy's linens in the same soap and water as a baronet's, the castle had one washroom for the court, and another adjoining it for those who served them. As always, the place was obscured by a fug of steam, and noisy with splashes, drips, and the hiss of irons. Pattern made her way past copper baths full of linens boiling in sudsy water, and through to where drying racks, operated by ropes and pulleys, dangled a forest of dripping cloth overhead. It was here she found a pile of clean uniforms set aside for mending, and picked up a Third Housemaid's heap of black flannel and white linen. With a bit of luck, the distraction of the banquet meant that she could return the clothes before they were missed.

The Grand Duchess was delighted with her costume, and Pattern had a hard time getting her to stand still long enough for her to stitch and pin it to an approximate fit. 'I think it must be exceedingly nice to have a uniform,' the Grand Duchess observed, 'and not to have the bothersome business of deciding what to wear three times a day.'

Her boots gave Pattern particular trouble, since their soft kid leather was far too fine for a servant. She took the oldest pair and dirtied them in the mud of the yard, trampling and scraping them as best she could. Then she bundled her mistress's hair under a white cap, pulling the brim so that it shaded her face, and stuck a basket into her hands.

'Keep your head down and follow me,' Pattern instructed, adjusting her bonnet and shawl, and feeling very nervous indeed. The Grand Duchess, of course,

would not get into trouble if they were found out, but the other servants would regard Pattern's actions as base treachery. They would move from slopping her tea to spitting in it.

The Grand Duchess was much impressed by the maze backstairs, and Pattern felt proud of her own competency in navigating it. Her mistress could scarce believe it when – after several twists and turns – they came out in the main passageway that went past the servants' hall to the kitchen. On the day of a state banquet it was filled with nearly as much heat and steam as the laundry rooms. The scents were overwhelming: roasting meats and stewing fruits, burnt sugar and scalded fat. Mrs Fischer and her assistants shouted orders; kitchen maids and boys scurried to obey. The Grand Duchess stood and stared, and when Pattern tugged her along, she stamped her foot. 'This is *my* kitchen. Why shouldn't I stay and watch a while?'

'You can inspect the kitchen whenever you wish – I'm sure your steward would be very pleased to give you the tour. But today you wish to pretend to be one of us.

You are either Highness, or you are Eleri. You cannot be both.'

The Grand Duchess's scowl turned into a sigh. 'I don't like being Highness much, in any event.'

Pattern remembered her moment of weakness with the gingerbread, when she had dreamed of another life as a pastry-cook. She softened her voice.

'This is a holiday for both of us. Let us make the most of it.'

With so many servants going hither and thither on so many errands, nobody thought to challenge them as they made their way out of the castle. Once under the cover of the wood, it was evident the Grand Duchess felt the same sense of release that Pattern had enjoyed on her own stolen afternoon. She skipped about and chattered away, and Pattern allowed herself to hope that perhaps the adventure would not end in disaster after all.

When they reached the marketplace, the Grand Duchess looked around her with as much wonder

as an ordinary girl might show on visiting London's zoological gardens. She was especially taken by a stall that sold patriotic souvenirs, and examined a wooden doll, made in her own image, with much amusement. 'Such pink cheeks! Such bright eyes and glossy curls! I fear I make for a very poor copy.' After shopping for supplies, she pronounced their meal of sausage and brown bread the best luncheon she had ever tasted. Then they took a stroll through the public park, and the Grand Duchess linked Pattern's arm in hers, the better to confide her distaste for the evening's festivities.

'Banquets are fearfully dull things: six courses of food, yet none of it very nice to eat, and so much speechifying that most of the guests have nodded off before pudding. The ladies are the worst. The husband-hunters make sheep's eyes at my uncle, because he is what passes for an eligible bachelor in these parts. And the married ones keep pushing their horrible chinless sons at me.'

'Surely you are a long way from marriage?'

'Marriage, yes; betrothal, no. No doubt my uncle is plotting a match that will be entirely to his advantage and not at all to mine.'

Pattern wished to avoid further talk of Prince Leopold. He might dislike his niece, but it was hard to believe in the villainy of a man whose chief delight was collectible figurines. As a distraction, she pointed to where a gang of urchins were dashing about under the trees. The group were baiting a boy wearing a snout made from a cone of paper. He rushed and roared at them, and if he managed to touch one of them on the head, the child would immediately drop to the ground.

Meanwhile, a solitary girl stood motionless on a bench, hands clasped as if in prayer, as her fellows tumbled around her.

'What are they playing, do you think?'

The Grand Duchess looked at the children and frowned. It was a grizzled gardener, who was weeding a flower bed beside them, who answered.

'They make a game of dragon-taming.' He shook his head. 'You'd think after recent happenings they'd have more care, but children can be heartless creatures.'

'Recent happenings?' the Grand Duchess asked sharply. 'Whatever do you mean?'

He looked surprised at the question. 'Why, the little ones who were taken, missy, out on the hills. And now they say another flock of sheep has been savaged too.'

The Grand Duchess gasped and put her hand to her mouth. She looked ready to faint. Pattern drew her away before the gardener could offer his assistance, and helped her mistress sit down on the rim of a raised pool. 'The children . . . the children . . .' she kept whispering.

'Such accidents are cruelly shocking,' Pattern

soothed. 'I myself felt quite unwell when I first heard. But you must recollect—'

'Wait. You *knew* of this?'

'The first time I went into town, people were talking of it.'

The Grand Duchess turned even paler. 'Tell me everything. At once. I command you!'

Pattern described what she had seen and heard. The Grand Duchess clenched her fists. Her face was so white and stretched that her cheekbones looked sharp enough to poke out from the skin. 'It is my uncle. I know it. He is even more cunning and ruthless than I dreamed.'

'Your uncle? How can he be involved?'

'He is abducting children, or worse, and setting it up in such a way that the people will believe the dragon has returned.'

Pattern felt as if she had missed a step on the stairs.

'Dragon? Forgive me: I do not understand.'

'The creature Prince Elffin brought with him from Wales,' the Grand Duchess said irritably. 'Elffin's

Bane. It is as the children were playing – the dragon comes out of its lair and attacks the country, until a princess is sacrificed to it. That is my uncle's plan, don't you see? He will arrange for more people to disappear, more crops to be wrecked and livestock taken, until the people demand my death to placate the monster. Just as they did to my poor forebears in the Hall of Maidens.'

Pattern's head whirled. 'But . . . your uncle cannot hope to deceive the people this way. No reasonable person would ever believe such a thing.'

'And why not?' the Grand Duchess asked sharply.

'Because . . . surely . . . I mean to say . . . we live in the *Modern Age*.' Until that moment, Pattern had never felt more of an Englishwoman, from the roots of her sensible hair to the toes of her sensible boots.

'What of my honoured ancestors, the sacrificial maidens of times past? How do you explain their fate?'

'Well, I do not know the particulars of their case,' Pattern said, as calmly as she was able, 'but in earlier times, people did not enjoy the scientific understanding that we have now. They relied on strange fancies to explain the world. Men of learning have since made studies of natural phenomena, and so put an end to many superstitions.' (Not all superstitions, of course. There was the market stall with its magical amulets, and Dilys's stories of the woman whose voice turned to slime, and the baby made of leaves. But now was hardly the time to mention it.) Pattern spoke more firmly still: 'This fear of dragons is surely born of the same ignorance that condemned so-called witches in times past. I am sure the good folk of Elffinberg will not stand for the Prince to fool them. They cannot be so credulous.'

The Grand Duchess looked at her inscrutably.

'You don't believe me. I think you must be in league with my uncle after all.'

'High— Eleri! No indeed—'

'*Yes*. I was a fool to trust you. All this time, you were merely pretending to dislike him and be a friend to me. Now you try to trick me into mistrusting my own mind, when I finally see the truth of his evil scheme.' Her voice rose, breathlessly. 'Did Prince Leopold tell

you to lure me out here, away from the protection of the castle? Because if I am discovered here – alone – defenceless – the people may try and kill me on the monster's behalf. I have no one to defend me – no one to listen to me – I will never be safe . . .'

All around, the gardens basked in the sun. Pigeons cooed, the children laughed at their game.

'You are safe with me, I promise you.' Pattern wanted to say, *Calm down, you are hysterical; you are making a spectacle of yourself.* But it was not her place. Even so, she reached out and tried to take the Grand Duchess's hand.

'Don't you *dare* touch me,' hissed the Grand Duchess. 'Or talk to me, or even look at me, ever again. You are dismissed.'

Then she snatched the keys from Pattern's basket, and ran off as if a whole herd of dragons were after her.

CHAPTER TEN

The persecutions and the ridicule of the world ought not to make us swerve a jot from truth and righteousness.

J. Bulcock, *The Duties of a Lady's Maid*

For a while, Pattern lacked the will to stir herself. She made no attempt to go after her mistress. Instead, she sat on the rim of the pool, face tilted towards the sun, and watched the children at their game. The little girl who played the Princess still kept her pose of martyrdom. Pattern found she did not like to see her wait so patiently, eyes glazed and hands clasped, as

the other urchins romped around.

It was possible the Grand Duchess would relent. It was probable, however, that she would not, and Pattern's short-lived career as a lady's maid was already over. She wondered how long it would be before Mrs Minchin learned of the fall of her star pupil. How the other girls at the Academy would crow if they could see her now! How Pol would sneer, and Sue would smirk!

She touched the pearl friendship brooch, and blushed at her own delusions. It had only ever been a vain fantasy that a servant girl could be friends with a princess. No, she must go back to always holding her tongue and hiding her thoughts and creeping about as meekly as a mouse. If she had only known her place, and kept to it, all this misery could have been avoided. She had only herself to blame.

A cold heaviness settled on Pattern's insides as she began to wonder how she was to get back to England. She had scarcely any money and no connections, and if forced to seek alternative employment in Elffinberg, she would have no references either. She had not even officially graduated from Mrs Minchin's Academy.

Yet it did not seem as dreadful as it might once have done to leave the Duchy in disgrace. Pleasant as the country was, one did not have to believe in fairy tales to sense there was also something crooked at its heart.

As Pattern made her way back through the wood, she walked in parallel to the gilded carriages clattering up the avenue. Those guests who would be spending the night had arrived some hours earlier and were dressing in their rooms. Soon all would gather to drink champagne on the terrace, with Prince Leopold as their host. The Grand Duchess had said she would not appear until the last possible moment, just before dinner was served.

Pattern was too proud to beg her way back into favour. Still, she felt she owed it to herself, as well as the Grand Duchess, to present herself for duty one final time. But when she made her way to the door of the royal apartment, a grinning page-boy informed her that Her Highness did not require her services. Now – or ever.

So that was that. She must inform the housekeeper of the situation, collect her wages and pack her things. She would allow herself only one indulgence: to look her last on the banqueting hall, where footmen were putting the finishing touches to the table. On damask linen tablecloths, the dazzling silver-gilt Grand Service was laid out in all its magnificence, burnished by candlelight. Lavish displays of Elffish porcelain lined the side tables; the Grand Duchess's place was flanked by candelabra four feet tall. Yet Pattern envied none of it. She would not regret it.

She turned and moved on, curiously light at heart.

'Miss. Please, miss . . .'

A soot-smudged maid was hastening towards her, holding out a handful of hairpins.

'Can you give these to the Countess of Brecon-Baden's woman? She said she needed them most pressingly, but we are all rushed off our feet, and there is already such a rumpus . . .'

She thrust the hairpins into Pattern's hands and was gone.

Pattern pursed her lips. She did not know the Countess or her maid, or where in the warren of guest rooms they might be staying, so she would have to find someone who did. Setting off on this final errand, she found her indignation grew. She was not, after all, entirely

accepting of her fate. Why should *she* take the blame? She had been whisked away from everything she was familiar with and set down in an inhospitable foreign land, whose noodle-brained Head of State had as good as accused her of treason. All the while, she had been a good and faithful servant. She did not deserve such treatment. Nobody did. It was an injustice! An insult! An outrage!

As her thoughts ran on, she hardly noticed she was walking through the castle in plain sight, as if she had every right to stride through its halls, rather than creep along its rat-runs.

Turning a corner, she spied the housemaid, Dilys, in conference with one of the evening's guests. He was a red-faced gentleman in a military uniform stuck all over with medals. His teeth were almost as shiny-yellow as his ornaments, and he flashed them in a near-continuous grin. Dilys, however, did not seem entirely comfortable. She kept her eyes down and held her body stiff.

Pattern continued towards them, but the light was dim and the carpet was soft, and they did not seem aware of her approach. The gentleman suddenly lunged forward, and tried to pull Dilys into an embrace. There was a moment of struggle, and an angry exclamation from Dilys. She wrested herself free and slapped the gentleman across the face.

Pattern was rooted to where she stood. The gentleman was redder than ever. His lips spluttered and his eyes bulged. But worse was to come, for strolling towards them from the other direction was Prince Leopold. 'Hallo, von Wynstein!' He took in the scene, and his twinkling smile grew fixed. 'Hey now, hey now, what's the to-do?'

Von Wynstein's splutters increased. 'I've never been so insulted in my life, that's what. Insulted *and* abused. Such gross impertinence.' He glared at Dilys, who was wan and trembling. 'I am quite overcome.'

'My dear fellow! I am appalled – outraged – mortified!' Indeed, the Prince's face was a picture of all these things. 'I can assure you the matter will be dealt with. Swiftly and severely, no less! I will give it my personal attention, I assure you. In the meantime,

let us turn our attention to happier pursuits. The night is young, old friend, and many pleasures beckon.'

The Prince ushered his guest through the doors at the end of the hall. He paused a moment, then returned to where Dilys was standing, her head bowed. His mouth was a thin line.

'Pack your bags and go.'

Dilys opened her mouth, but no words came. All the snap had gone out of her. Her shoulders slumped.

It was then Pattern stepped out of the shadows. 'Highness, if I might speak to you a moment . . . ?'

Irritation twitched through the Prince's person. However, he looked at her again, and managed an affable smile. 'Aha! It's the little maid who is tending to my niece. What can I do for you, child?'

'Please, Your Highness, Dilys is a very modest, respectable girl. I was witness to her encounter with the gentleman, and I can testify that she did nothing wrong. I am afraid . . . that is, I fear the gentleman's attentions to her were not as they should have been.'

'Is that so? Hm. You put me in a delicate situation,

child. Delicate and difficult! The gentleman in question is a dear friend of mine.'

'In the servants' hall, Highness, there is much talk of what a kind and liberal master you are. You have a great many friends of rank, but I think you enjoy the love of the common people too. I am sure you would not like to lose it.'

Despite the steadiness of her voice, her palms were sweating. She had never dreamed she could be so bold. But then she had already lost her position. She only sought to keep Dilys from losing hers.

Prince Leopold stared long and hard. 'You think I don't know how to keep the loyalty of the people?' This time his eyes were not so merry, and his smile not quite so twinkling.

'You should remember that you are Elffish born, if not raised. I expect loyalty from you also.'

'Oh yes, Your Highness.' Pattern's face was bland as a bowl of milk. 'The Grand Duchess will always be able to trust in me. I can promise you that.'

CHAPTER ELEVEN

According to the confidence which is reposed in you, it is probable that you may be entrusted with secrets of various kinds . . . it is of the utmost consequence to your character that they may be kept inviolable.

J. Bulcock, *The Duties of a Lady's Maid*

Twisting about on her lumpy mattress, Pattern could not account for why she had meddled in matters that did not concern her, on behalf of people who wished her gone. Since she had been unable to find Mrs Parry, she did not even know whether she would be granted a few days' grace, or if she would be booted out of the castle at first light. Eventually she fell into a fitful doze. She dreamed of roads unfurling through a tangled wood, of gingerbread houses and china dolls with knives for teeth. The teeth made a grinding sound.

The grinding increased. It was her doorknob, turning.

'Who's there?' she called out, sitting up in bed.

Heavy breathing. Creaking floorboards; a spill of candlelight. A hooded figure slipped through the door.

Pattern prepared to brandish her water jug . . .

'Shh! It's me!'

'Your *Highness*?' The thumping of Pattern's heart slowed. 'Whatever are you doing here?'

'Dilys told me how you stood firm against Prince Leopold. You saved her position, and avowed your loyalty to me. Me! Who abused and insulted you, and would have turned you out of the door! I am so ashamed, Pattern. I have been an unworthy monarch and an even worse friend. Can you forgive me?'

Under the cloak, the Grand Duchess was still

wearing her evening finery. Candlelight gleamed on the rich scarlet folds of her gown, and caught at the rope of pearls and diamonds around her neck. But the curls were already coming out of her hair, her face was as pinched and shadowed at is had ever been, and the grandeur of her costume looked absurd for so young a girl. A lonely little girl, frightened of monsters under the bed . . . Pattern felt old beyond her years. Old and tired. She saw how life was always going to be: the Grand Duchess all fury one moment and sweetness the next, with Pattern standing by to humour and soothe, mending hurts as expertly as she darned stockings . . . Was this what friendship meant?

'Forgive me. Please,' said the Grand Duchess again, and put her cold hand on Pattern's.

Pattern tried to smile. 'Yes, Your Highness. As you wish.'

'You must call me Eleri – now and for always. I wish us to be true friends, and that means we must be equals.'

'I am not sure that's possible,' Pattern said, as gently

as she was able. 'Society and culture and custom forbid it. My position—'

'Hang your position! It's your *character* I care for. I see your true value, and I hope you will come to know mine, though I fear there's much that needs improving. This friendship business is harder work that I realized. But we will learn how to do it together, and practise as we go. That is . . . if you are willing to try?'

Pattern's smile came more easily this time. 'I am not afraid of hard work.'

'No, you must not be afraid.' The Grand Duchess sat on the bed and gnawed her lip. Her eyes had a hectic glitter. 'I know you to be clever and good; I hope you are brave also. It may be that I *am* losing my mind. But I plan to show you my secret, so that you will understand why. You must trust me, and stay strong. Can you do that?'

Pattern nodded. Exciting and alarming things were about to happen, and to her surprise, she wanted to be part of it.

'Then put on your boots and follow me. Quickly now!'

Pattern dressed hurriedly. The clock on her desk showed it to be approaching three o'clock as the two girls crept out of the room. The Grand Duchess – or Eleri, as Pattern must try to think of her – held up her candle, illuminating the row of little wooden doors repeating down the length of the attic hallway. 'I thought I should never find my way up here,' she whispered. 'Yours was the third door I tried, but the other inmates were snoring so soundly I should think they'd sleep through an earthquake.'

The immensity of the castle meant that much of it lay deserted even in the busiest hours of the day. There were not footmen enough to be stationed at half the doors, and not courtiers enough to grace more than a handful of reception rooms. At this time of night, it was easy to believe they were the only creatures to inhabit the place.

Pattern was not entirely surprised to find their destination was the library. Even though no one was likely to be browsing the shelves at this hour, Eleri insisted they check every corner before proceeding to the hidden door that led to the Old Castle. But instead of climbing the stairs up to the Hall of Maidens, Eleri turned the other way. It turned out the stairs went further down. They became yet steeper, taking them deep under the castle, below even the cellars. There was another ancient door at the bottom, to which Eleri applied a little gold key. It led to a small chamber furnished as a chapel, with a plain stone altar and a very worn Celtic cross.

The walls were covered with the remains of blotched and faded frescoes. They depicted the adventures of a man with red hair and a yellow crown; Prince Elffin, Pattern presumed. Here he was, climbing a hill . . . sailing through a storm . . . leading an army . . . addressing a crowd. Several of the frescoes looked to have been deliberately scratched out; others were entirely baffling. Pattern peered at one that showed the Prince standing before the rising sun with his arms uplifted. The next depicted him kneeling by a fire, with a snake, a bell, a knife and several other strange objects around him.

His descendant was also kneeling, but before the

cross, her lips moving in soundless prayer. Then she lit a fresh candle from a bundle in a corner of the room and moved to the wall opposite the altar. Unlike the others, it looked to be sheer rock. Eleri ran her fingers over its rough surface, until she hooked her finger on a crack that Pattern was sure was so small it could not be seen, only felt.

'Ta-dah!'

At her touch, there was a clicking sound, and the crack grew and widened, until the gap was just large enough to step through. Pattern did not know what she expected to find beyond. Some treasure-trove, perhaps, or an alchemist's laboratory. Instead, all that was revealed was a downward-sloping passageway.

'Does it lead to the dungeons?' Pattern ventured.

'A dungeon of sorts!'

Eleri picked up her skirts and set off. Pattern followed more slowly, through the flare of candlelight and plunging darkness, feeling the weight of the rock press down all around. Her breathing grew light and rapid; her heart leaped awkwardly against her ribs.

They continued in silence for what felt like a long time but what was probably no more than a quarter of an hour. The passage became steadily rougher and more tunnel-like, though Eleri swept along confidently enough. At least the mystery of her torn slippers and soiled nightgowns was now answered. Suddenly she came to a halt. 'We are nearly there,' she whispered. 'The passage forks just ahead. The right-hand path will take us up and out; the left leads to an iron grate. I want you to go ahead and look through the grate, keeping quiet all the while.' She paused. 'Pattern, are you ready for this?'

'Yes, Highness. Eleri, I mean.'

'Will you be strong? Will you be steadfast?'

'I – I will do my best.'

Eleri seized her hand and squeezed it so hard Pattern's fingers cramped. There was fear in the girl's face, but also a feverish excitement that Pattern was almost more unsettled by. She paused a moment, waiting until her pulse had calmed, before she took the candle and proceeded down the left turn of the tunnel.

It was not long before she saw the rusting grate. Just beyond, the passage ended in a narrow ledge. The drop was very steep. Pattern would have thought it would be cold down here, so far beneath the ground, but in fact the air was close and warm, with a thickly sulphurous smell. Eleri's rapid breathing in the passageway behind was curiously amplified, or else it was her own breath that was suddenly echoing all around.

She moved a step closer to the grate. A shaft of bluish moonlight slanted down from some fissure far above. It revealed a cavern as lofty as a cathedral. The ground below appeared to be made up of undulating hillocks, and spiky shards of rock. It was black as tar, with an oily rainbow sheen.

There was a great echoing sigh, and the ground heaved and twitched. With a jolt of horror, Pattern realized it was not rock that twitched, nor earth that moved – the black tar was in fact the shining, sliding scales of a vast, coiled creature: something spiky yet serpentine. A tarry black lid rolled back and she stared into the hot yellow slit of an eye. It was filmy,

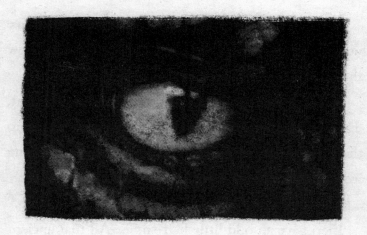

unfocused. The next instant the lid drooped closed, and the creature let out another vast, bubbling snore.

Pattern stood very still, gripping hold of the candlestick, as all the hairs lifted on the back of her neck. She scarcely dared breathe, let alone move. The urge to scream was swelling inside her, bulging in her throat, until it threatened to burst through all defences. It felt as if even her bones began to shake. So she clenched her jaw, hard enough to make her teeth ache, and took one step back. Then another. And another, until the horror was out of sight, and she and Eleri were once more enclosed in the empty dark.

'What *is* that?' Pattern had waited until her voice was almost steady again, but in truth she already knew the answer.

'Elffin's Bane.' Eleri's face flickered in the candlelight. 'Even the thought of it is enough to strike terror into the heart of any man. But is there not something wondrous, too, about such a sight?'

'I – I don't know.'

Eleri gave an odd little half-smile. 'All that ancient strength and heat and fury, lying quietly beneath the rock . . . Yes, I think it is as much a marvel as a monster. I come to watch it sleep, you see, and wonder what it dreams. Of the death of princesses, perhaps, and the long-lost hills of Wales; of rising up to beat its wings against the sky, and raking its claws through our green earth. Perhaps it even dreams of me.'

Instead of returning the way they came, Eleri took the right-hand fork in the passageway. It ended in another flight of twisting stairs. They led up to a grotto in the castle grounds. 'This door only gets you out; it does not open the other way,' Eleri explained. 'Our passages are too small for the beast to squeeze through, but there is a tunnel that leads from its lair all the way up to the mountains, which is how the dragon has come and gone in times past.'

She put her eye to a spy-hole cut in the wall at the top of the stairs, before pressing a hidden catch. A spring clicked and a panel of stone swung open. In moments, they were standing in an artificial cave, decorated all over with shells, flints and coloured glass.

They sat on the steps of the grotto and looked out over the gardens. Dawn was just breaking; the avenues were shrouded in autumn mist, the lawns pearly with dew. Everything seemed made of shadows.

'Are you sorry I showed you?' Eleri asked presently. 'Sometimes I fancy it is all a feverish dream. I imagine I will awake to find my papa is still alive, and there is no dragon, and I have not a care in the world.'

Pattern did not know how to reply. Rationally, she *should* have been a shivering, gibbering wreck. Her sensible and tidy mind *should* have shut down in shock.

Yet she felt more clear-eyed and alert than she ever had in her life. She began to understand the unwholesome excitement of such a secret.

'How . . . how did you discover the thing?'

'I grew up with the story of Elffin's Bane. Everyone here does. I never guessed about the secret passage, though, and what is waiting at the end of it. Papa only told me when he was sick, and knew he was not going to get better. All down the generations, the reigning Grand Duke or Duchess has entrusted the truth of the passage to their heir, swearing them to secrecy.' Her mouth quirked. 'I must be the first in line to have broken that promise.'

'And your uncle? What does he know?'

'Only the tale of a monster who came out from the mountains to ravage the land, but has not been seen or heard of in over a hundred years. You see, the dragon is very old, perhaps sick, and spends its time sleeping. Most people presume it has died, or else they think as you did: that it was only ever a tale or superstition. Certainly, if my uncle has his way, it will make no difference to anyone whether there is a real live dragon or not. The result is just the same. The children will still be taken, the crops and flocks still destroyed, and I will still be sacrificed so that Prince Leopold can take the throne.'

'I can scarcely believe it myself,' said Pattern, 'even though I have looked on the creature with my own eyes.' She kept her hands folded neatly in her lap in case they should start trembling. 'Can you tell me how the dragon came to be?'

Eleri sighed. 'I will give you the same account my papa told me. For he said that in ancient times there may have been a number of such creatures about the earth. However, Wales was their last known dwelling place, and ours is the last of its kind. Prince Elffin found it one day when he was wandering the mountainside. It was newly hatched, and very small. A mere wyrmling. So the Prince took it with him into exile, and used it to frighten away rival claimants for this land. That was when he took the name *Pendraig* – it means 'Chief Dragon', you know. It was said he had a magical

incantation to command the beast. Perhaps you saw the picture in the chapel frescoes – some business with bells and bones and other talismans.

'Well, however it was supposed to work, his magic did not hold. Dragons grow very fast, and this one soon became too strong and dangerous, and escaped its captor. After creating all sorts of mischief, it flew away into the mountains. There it burrowed deep within the rock, till it found or made a nest for itself below the fortress where Elffin had once imprisoned it.

'But it did not stay hidden for long. It came out, and laid the country to waste. There was terrible suffering. Children were always the prime victims; they are the right size for carrying off, I suppose, and their flesh is more tender. Yet only one thing would satisfy the beast's hunger: the death of a Princess. For the blood of Royal Maidens is like an opiate to dragon-kind – a powerful drug, and irresistible delight. And so Elffin's granddaughter was its first sacrifice. She was fifteen years old when she offered herself up, willingly, to save the people. The dragon slaked its thirst on her blood, and slept for nearly twenty years. The people rejoiced. But then it woke, and was thirsty again . . .'

Pattern shivered. In the cold dawn light, the gardens seemed ashen and desolate as any underworld.

Eleri gave a small, bleak smile. 'Ours is a small country. We keep ourselves to ourselves. Yet there have always been rumours that Elffinberg is in possession of a secret, most unholy weapon. It is why no enemy has ever crossed our borders to try and steal our riches or our lands. It is why we have been untroubled by war. It is why the crown has passed quietly from one generation to the next. It is the price of our peace.'

CHAPTER TWELVE

Another requisite of attention is an observant eye.

J. Bulcock, *The Duties of a Lady's Maid*

The Grand Duchess told Pattern that she was going to bed, and did not intend to rise before tea-time. She suggested that Pattern do the same. By the time they had parted ways back at the castle, it was close to five, and the youngest and lowliest of the lower servants were already astir. There were chamber-pots to empty, floors to mop and shoes to clean; fires needed to be laid in bedroom grates and water set to boil on kitchen ranges.

'There you are!'

It was Dilys, clattering up the backstairs with a box of blacking bottles and brushes. 'Well, you're the mouse that roared, and no mistake! I don't know how you dared be so saucy with the Prince, but I owe you a deal of thanks.'

'And I wanted to thank you, too, for speaking to Her Highness—'

'Oh, never mind that. I've a sharp tongue, and I'm sorry if you've felt the sting of it. But have no fear: from here on, if there's folk who want to make mischief for you, they'll have me to answer to.' She rattled her blacking box for emphasis. 'Franz as well. He's a coachman, and my particular friend. I'm sure you'll have seen him in the stable yard – he's by far the handsomest person there, so you can't miss him. I've told him to look out for you too.'

Pattern was glad to know she had some allies in the castle, but even Dilys was no match for the troubles massing ahead. She wanted only to rest her aching head, to gather her thoughts somewhere quiet . . .

'I am surprised to find you up at this hour, Miss Pattern.'

'I could say the same of you, Mr Madoc.'

'Well, you know what they say about early birds.' The man was an aniseed-scented smile in the shadows. 'And this castle is certainly full of worms.'

Pattern made to move past, but found the way blocked.

'My master the Prince is disappointed. He was expecting to hear from you, as regards the well-being of his niece.'

'There has been nothing to report, since I am happy to say she is in excellent health.'

'Indeed! Perhaps this accounts for her newfound passion for vengeance.'

'I – I'm afraid I don't follow.'

'Your play, Miss Pattern. *The Butler's Revenge*? I was hoping that you might also favour me with a recitation. I am sure I would find it highly informative.'

Pattern pursed her lips, and once again tried to move past. Once again, he moved to block her. This time his way of speaking was as politely earnest as when they had first met. 'Do not mistake me, Miss Pattern. I must follow my orders, the same as you, but be assured I am my own man. In turbulent times, you'll find downstairs collaboration is every bit as rewarding as upstairs diplomacy. I can be a both good and useful friend.'

'I'm sure you're right, Mr Madoc, but I am starting to learn that friendship in this castle always comes at a price.' Pattern drew a slightly shaky breath. 'Now, if you'll excuse me, I must be getting on.'

She was sure that if she was detained a moment longer she would blurt out all manner of fears and furies. This sprawling stone pile, in which so many people lived and worked, might as well have been built from straw. A nightmare lurked beneath, with a furnace in its belly, and jaws rusted with ancient blood. It seemed as if the beast had only to turn in its sleep, for the whole castle to quake. She fancied she could smell the sulphurous whiff of its breath seeping up through the gutters.

At least she now understood why her parents had fled the country. They must have been afraid of the

dragon and fearful for the safety of their newborn child. It was some comfort to know their motivation at last, and she felt a glow of warmth for their resolve, as well as admiration for the risk they had taken. Yet little good the enterprise had done them! For here she was, back in the dragon's den . . .

Now she came to think of it, signs of the beast were everywhere. Its likeness fluttered on flags, was baked into the decorative crusts of pies, enamelled on brooches, carved into wood and etched on glass. These representations were mostly handsome and heraldic in style, with no hint of the bloodthirsty reality. Perhaps the Elffish thought if they flattered the beast it would treat them more gently. It was possible they took a peculiar kind of pride in their secret.

As she closed the door of her room behind her, she was sure rest would be impossible. *Perhaps it even dreams of me*, the Grand Duchess had said. A most unwelcome thought struck her: could the beast be communing with the Grand Duchess in her sleep? Was this the reason for her strange voices and even stranger declamations, her trance-like state? Pattern remembered how Eleri had turned her uncannily blank gaze upon her in the night, and those hissed words of mysterious threat:

Little girl. Stranger from a strange land. I see you too. You are watching and waiting, and so am I. You are not afraid yet, but you will be.

Did this mean the dragon had spoken to *her*, too?

Despite everything, Pattern managed to sleep for a couple of hours, rising just after eleven, when she made her way downstairs in the hope of finding something to eat. The kitchens should have been all a-hubbub with preparations for luncheon. Yet the place was curiously subdued. A knot of people were crowding around one of the under-cooks, who was weeping into her apron.

'It's her nephew,' one hall-boy told another, in hushed tones. 'He was helping his older brother harvest fruit at Caer Grunwald. But he grew bored and wandered off to explore. There was a great thundering and rumbling. When he didn't come back, the brother went to look for him. All he found was a burnt patch in the grass, and a couple of buttons from the lad's jacket.'

Pattern felt a knot tighten in her stomach. Many questions came to mind, though none of them were fitting at such at time. Moreover, it occurred to her that, as the Grand Duchess's maid, it would not do for her to appear too interested in such events. So she moved quietly away, pocketing a stray meat pie as she did so, as well as a well-thumbed copy of the *Elffish Enquirer* that somebody had left on a chair.

For all Eleri's constant speculation about her uncle and his schemes, she showed little interest in the world outside the castle gates. Perhaps she was afraid of it. She preferred the fashion periodicals to newspapers, which she avowed were full of lies. However, it occurred to Pattern

that even if the *Enquirer* merely repeated the tattle of the marketplace, it would still be a valuable informant.

And so it proved. Reading the paper, Pattern learned that in addition to the under-cook's nephew, a total of twenty children had disappeared over the last two months. The victims were aged between seven and ten, and had been alone in the countryside at the time of their disappearance. In each case, all that remained of the poor souls was a patch of smoking ground and a few sad relics – a shoe, a buckle, a hank of singed hair. There were no witnesses to what had befallen them, but the charred and torn carcasses of sheep and cattle had been recovered nearby, and great claw marks found gouged in the earth. Farmers reported the burning of crops, and rumours abounded of strange flashes in the sky, billowing 'winged clouds' and rumbles like thunder.

The newspaper's editors seemed, for the moment, reluctant to name the suspicion that must lurk in their readers' minds. Veiled references to 'old troubles' and the return of 'dark times' were as far as they went. Even so, Pattern was shocked that things had already come

to such a pass. No wonder people whispered in corners. No wonder people were afraid.

And now that she knew there was, in fact, a real live dragon, she could not blame them. Pattern wondered if Eleri was right to think the beast was too old and weary to leave its lair. Yet the fact there were no eye-witnesses to any of the attacks struck her as strange.

Since the Grand Duchess was still in bed, Pattern resolved to make some enquiries of her own. To this end, she changed her lady's-maid finery for an old work-smock she had worn in Mrs Minchin's Academy, and set off to find a way of getting to Caer Grunwald. She wished to examine the scene of the crime for herself.

Pattern was in luck – the man who had brought the news of the under-cook's nephew had not yet left the castle. She found him eating bread and cheese in the stable yard, having delivered his bad news along with a consignment of apples for the kitchen. Putting on her best approximation of an Elffish accent, she asked if he was returning to Caer Grunwald, and if so, could she journey with him on the cart? 'It is my afternoon off,' she explained. 'And I promised to visit my aunt, who is working in the orchards.'

'I'll be glad to give you a ride, little miss. But don't stray from the fields, and keep close to your friends. We don't want anyone else coming to harm.'

In other circumstances Pattern, who had thought to spend her whole life in a maze of smoke stacks and dirty brick, would have enjoyed the expedition. The valley of Caer Grunwald had the ideal climate for growing fruit, and in spring the acres of orchards, snowy with blossom, were one of Elffinberg's finest sights. Pattern gazed in wonder at the avenues of apple, pear and plum trees laden with produce, and the harvesters who swarmed around them as purposefully as bees.

Her driver had needed little encouragement to repeat his account of tragedy. He even pointed out the path the missing child had taken. Once he had pulled up the cart, and his workfellows were occupied with loading it, Pattern slipped away from the orchards and into the hills. After nearly an hour's walk, the path meandered down

to a small wooded gorge. There was a clearing in the middle, scarred by a shallow crater about two feet wide. The grass all around was burnt black. Not far along, giant scratch marks had been gouged from the ground.

Standing out in the sun, it was hot and very still. The only sound was the dry rustling of the trees. There was a faint smell of eggs gone bad, or mud flats at low tide. As Pattern picked her way across the scorched earth, flies circled lazily about her head. She began to wonder exactly how far she had come and, if she were to suffer a misadventure, how long it would be before she was missed.

She swallowed hard and resolved to concentrate on the task in hand. In the alarm and distress of the initial discovery it was quite possible some clue had been overlooked. She did not know what to make of the fact that all that was left of the child was a couple of buttons. If one was to believe the dragon was responsible, this would suggest the boy had either been carried off elsewhere – perhaps even to the lair under the castle – or else had been burnt to nothingness by the same fire-blast that had made the crater. But until a body, or the remains of a body, was found, it was possible to hope he was still alive.

Pattern bent to retie her laces, and her eye was caught by a plum stone lying on the ground. She would have thought it was a bit of pebble, but for its yellowish sheen. There were no fruit trees in the wood.

A little further along she found another plum stone nestled in the grass. Then another. Pattern moved deeper into the trees. She pictured the child sneaking off from his labours and loading his pockets with stolen plums. Rather than spitting out the stones, he kept them as trophies. Perhaps he intended to make a game of them. And then, having been taken captive, he threw them out of his pocket to leave a trail . . .

The trail ended in something equally interesting: boot marks and trampled grass. A wisp of yellow hair.

Pattern felt a lifting of her heart. The driver had described the lad in sentimental detail, including the golden curls that had been his mother's pride and joy. Now it seemed he had not been taken without a fight.

Much encouraged, she combed the area for further signs of the scuffle. At first, she did not know what to make of a frayed bit of cord she spied in the roots of an elder, but she put it in her pocket just in case. Then she found a torn scrap of brown paper in a bramble bush. It bore what looked like a Chinese character.

Pattern's formal education might be sadly lacking, but the Academy's single-volume encyclopaedia had nonetheless provided a ready supply of facts and figures. Madoc had deemed facts dull in comparison to fairy tales, but Pattern had always found the accumulation of them a great comfort. From the encyclopaedia's entry on China, she knew that the Chinese were renowned for three great inventions: printing, pyrotechnics and porcelain. Prince Leopold himself had reminded her of the latter. In fact, he had even boasted of his close association with a Chinese personage of high rank. Might his love of porcelain have led him to an interest in pyrotechnics also?

She considered the crater. It was possible the piece of cord had been used as a fuse to light an explosive.

Witnesses had reported sounds like thunder, which might sound like a dragon's roar, but was almost certainly the rumble of an explosion. It would surely take a very little quantity of gunpowder to create the hole she had seen. Claw-marks were easy to stage-manage; so too were the savaged cattle and burnt crops.

Pattern knew she had little in the way of proof. A handful of plum stones and a wisp of hair were nothing in themselves, and a scrap of foreign packaging and bit of cord did not add up to anything much. Yet it was enough to convince her that Eleri was right. The only monsters at work were human ones. They must have been watching the orchards, waiting for a child to move away from the safety of the group. Then they had followed him through the trees to a place where no one would hear his cries . . .

She made her way back to the clearing, deep in thought. But she was no longer alone. Two men were standing there, wearing the livery of Prince Leopold's personal guard.

'What are you doing here?' barked the elder, who

bristled with a most fearsome moustache. 'This is a crime scene, not a picnicking spot.'

Pattern begged pardon, hoping that her surprise did not detract from the accuracy of her Elffish lilt, and that her down-turned face remained hidden by her bonnet. She began to back away.

'It's not safe to wander the countryside alone,' the other fellow said, narrowing his eyes. 'Surely you know that. Where are you from? What do you know of the attack?'

'I don't know anything, sir. I'm very sorry. I – I'll leave at once.'

'How old are you, girl?'

'Wait a while!'

They called out something else, but she was already scurrying away through the trees. Her heart did not stop pounding until she was back in the orchards. The orderly avenues, the scent of warm grass and ripeness, were lovelier than ever in the late afternoon light. Yet as Pattern picked her way past the windfalls and wasps, she caught in the air's sweetness a rotten taint.

CHAPTER THIRTEEN

⚬ ⚬

Sickness, danger, and adversity, usually level distinctions of rank.

J. Bulcock, *The Duties of a Lady's Maid*

⚬ ⚬

Pattern found her way into a covered wagon filled with fruit-pickers bound for home. Most were too weary to talk, their backs aching and noses sun-burned, fingers and clothes stained with juice. Pattern, who had eaten nothing all day but the meat pie and a couple of bruised plums, was as hungry as she was footsore by the time she reached Elffinheim's walls. However, as she limped

along the road to the castle, she was surprised to find herself part of a stream of people. A jostling, muttering crowd had gathered outside the gates.

It was composed of both country folk and townspeople, and the mood was ugly. 'Come out and show yourselves,' one of the ringleaders shouted. 'Our children have been taken, our livelihoods destroyed. And still no word from our royal masters!'

'For shame,' others cried. 'Cowards!'

Pattern, lurking on the edge of the crowd, could

see very little but the backs of people's heads. There was a new kind of commotion at the entrance to the avenue, and shouts from the sentry-men. She feared the roughness of the protesters had spilt over, and that the demonstration was about to turn violent.

'Fellow countrymen! Honest citizens! Friends and neighbours! Peace, I beg of you. Peace!'

Prince Leopold. This was interesting. He was greeted with as many jeers as cheers, yet his voice rang out confidently.

'Be assured that we in the Royal Household are not insensible of your plight. Not in the slightest! It pains us grievously.'

'Then where's the Grand Duchess?' somebody yelled. 'Did she send you because she's too spineless to face us herself?'

Some applauded, but others shook their heads. 'Why, she's nothing but a child,' said one old lady.

'She's still our Head of State,' another retorted. 'And she should know there's a price to be paid for sitting cosy in the castle, eating peacock pie off a golden plate.'

'Shh!' said another. 'Let the Prince speak!'

'I have come here to tell you,' said the Prince, once the rumblings of the crowd had subsided, 'that I will personally compensate each and every one of you who has suffered hardship as the result of an attack on your livestock or crops. Give your name to my man here, and we'll do our utmost to put things right. Furthermore, if any of you were witness to these scenes of carnage, or have any additional information to supply, you will be amply rewarded. Very amply!'

Pattern stood on tiptoe and craned her neck. She glimpsed Madoc, looking graver than ever, wielding a notebook and pencil at his master's side.

Now Prince Leopold's voice grew slow and heavy. Pattern did not need to see the gentleman to picture the tears of emotion in his eyes. They welled up moistly through every word. 'Dear, *dear* friends. I know that the loss of children is a blow beyond compare. Nothing can compensate. Nothing can ease the pain. All I can say is this: we will leave no stone unturned in our quest to discover the fate of your little ones. No stone, no twig, not even a pebble! My own guard have been tasked with investigating these incidents, under my personal supervision.' He paused impressively. 'Rest assured, we – that is, the Grand Duchess Arianwen and myself – will do whatever necessary to curtail this threat. However high the cost, however bitter the blow. *Whatever necessary.* You have my word. Thank you, and a very good night!'

His departure was accompanied by a storm of exclamation and excitement. Many of the crowd surged forward to surround Madoc and his pencil.

'Elffinberg is fortunate to have such a Prince,' exclaimed a whiskery woman standing next to Pattern. 'As wise a counsellor as he is generous a master.'

'Are you in the Prince's employ?' Pattern asked curiously.

'I'm his housekeeper,' the woman replied with pride. 'That is, I have the care of his hunting lodge. However, it has lately been shut up, for at the first rumour of an attack, my kind master closed the house and sent all of the servants to shelter within the town. He has

promised to pay for our keep until the danger is passed, and the remote countryside is safe again.'

'This lodge . . . it is in an isolated spot?'

'It is not so very far from here, but deep in the Forest of Annwn. If the dragon should strike, we'd have little chance of rescue.'

Although Pattern had thought herself prepared, it still came as a shock to hear the threat named so plainly. 'Surely we cannot be certain what – or who – the culprit is. The evidence is entirely circumstantial. Nobody has actually *seen* the creature.'

'Ah, but they have, you know. More reports are coming in by the day – of plumes of fire, almighty roars and the flapping of great black wings.'

Pattern feared this was likely to be true. As the hysteria mounted, people of a nervous disposition would imagine they spied monsters everywhere. Moreover, if Madoc and his master were rewarding witnesses with money, there would be plenty of rogues ready to swear to seeing whatever they asked.

The whiskery housekeeper shook her head. 'Small

wonder the Grand Duchess has been hiding away for all these weeks. I wouldn't like to be in her shoes right now, for all their satin trimmings.'

Eleri was indeed in hiding, having overheard from a footman of the demonstration outside the gates. Pattern found her huddled in the back of her wardrobe, quaking under a pile of furs. 'They'll storm the castle the next time,' she said, 'and come for me with pitchforks and knives.'

Pattern offered what comfort she could. 'I have found – if not absolute proof – strong evidence that whatever is happening to the children and the farmland has been done by human hands. As soon as the people realize this, they will be reasonable again.'

She related her discoveries, but Eleri hardly listened. 'Yes, yes,' she said impatiently, throwing off the furs. 'I already told you it was my uncle. I do not see why you had to go gallivanting all over the countryside to find that out.'

'But I am near certain the missing children are alive.

Your uncle is not wicked enough to murder them. Surely that is good news?'

'He still means to murder *me*. For how else will he claim the throne?' Eleri stared at Pattern. 'Do you know what happens to princesses who are fed to the dragon? They are dressed all in white and led in solemn procession to a patch of wasteland, high in the mountains. And there they are chained to a rock, and left for the dragon to tear them to pieces. I wonder how much of me my uncle will leave as evidence of my fate. Perhaps a finger; perhaps a foot. Or an eye.'

Pattern suppressed a shudder. 'It will not come to that,' she said firmly. 'We will find the stolen children, and so prove the dragon is not to blame. Then the country must unite to find a way of putting an end to the beast once and for all. With all the technological advances of recent years, I am sure something can be done. Modern weaponry—'

'Bullets would simply bounce off the thing. A dragon's hide is practically armour-plated.'

'Then we could try poison gases. Or use explosives

'to blow it up in its lair.'

'But my castle would blow up with it!'

'You can always build a new one.' Something well-appointed and modern, Pattern thought, with half as many stairs, and decent quarters for the servantry. 'Tell me: Prince Leopold already enjoys wealth and influence, so why is he intent on stealing your throne? I do not doubt his motives,' she added hastily. 'I merely seek to understand them better.'

'Well, he is greedy for power, like all tyrants. But he is also greedy in the more common way. He lost a deal of money investing in some foolish scheme to enhance the manufacture of porcelain, and then yet more in improving his country estate. Consequently he is not nearly so rich as he was, nor half as rich as he believes he ought to be. His great ambition is to swank about the royal courts of Europe, boring all the other poor monarchs to tears with tales of his wretched pots. He might manage this as a Grand Duke, but he has little chance as an impoverished princeling.'

Pattern rubbed her nose thoughtfully. 'Is this country

estate separate from the Prince's hunting lodge?'

'Oh yes. It lies by the northern mountains, which are even craggier than the ones here, and covered in snow half the year. But the lodge is in the forest by the spa town of Llanotto Wells, some thirty miles from Elffinheim. I have only been there once, when Papa was still alive, but my uncle is there often. He likes killing animals almost as much as he likes fondling pots.'

'I heard that the lodge has been all shut up, and its servants sent away.'

It had struck Pattern that if Prince Leopold was planning to fake a dragon, he would need a headquarters suited to the task. His apartments in the castle were always abuzz with the comings-and-goings of friends and cronies, servants and supplicants. An empty house in the middle of a forest was far more practicable.

She explained her reasoning to Eleri. 'If we can be sure the Prince is not at the lodge, we must contrive a way to visit it. Perhaps the stolen children are imprisoned there. Perhaps we will find other proof of his misdeeds.'

'It is certainly worth trying.' Yet Eleri did not look particularly hopeful. 'You know, Pattern, if the dragon were to rise again, I *would* give myself to it. I am horribly afraid to die, and I do not like the people very much, yet I know my duty. I could not sit back as they were slaughtered in their fields.'

Pattern did not know what to say to this. She tried to steer the conversation back to more practical matters. 'The Prince's plot—'

'The Prince's plot may yet succeed,' Eleri said flatly. 'So if we do not find the children, or some other evidence of my uncle's crimes, I must go to him and give him the crown of my own free will, and he will have to find some other explanation for these so-called attacks.'

'You . . . you mean to abdicate?'

Eleri hunched her thin shoulders. 'Well, it is better than having my throat slit to placate a dragon – imaginary or otherwise. I shall be the last true duchess of Elffinberg, in any event.'

*

That night, Pattern dreamed of the dragon. She dreamed of rising from her bed and creeping down the narrow passage through the rock. She dreamed of standing by the iron grate, watching the monster sleep.

In her dream, she put her hand through the bars, and stroked the creature's rusting scales. The heat of it beat through her flesh, so that her body throbbed with it, and her bones quaked in time to the pulse of its heart.

'Little girl,' it said. 'Little stranger. I have tasted your scent, now, and weary as I am, I feel the old hunger rising. I feel the old hunger, and I hear a new call!'

Then it opened its eyes, and this time there was no film of sleep upon them, only fury and fire, white-hot as the core of the sun, and rimmed with the blackness of an infinite night.

CHAPTER FOURTEEN

You must consider that your employers like to have things done their own way.

J. Bulcock, *The Duties of a Lady's Maid*

A Grand Duchess needed to account for her time in much the same way as a lady's maid. A few stolen hours were one thing; a whole day's absence quite another, for which she needed the approval of her guardian as well as the company of a chaperone. Accordingly, Eleri applied to her uncle for permission to travel to the von Bliven estate to pay her respects to her godmama's heir.

Prince Leopold was in a self-important whirl of bustle, for the Prince Elffin's Day Ball was a mere five days away, and he had taken all its organization upon himself. Whether he was distracted or unwilling or both, he did not approve his niece's plans until late the next evening. In the meanwhile, Eleri and Pattern spent a long afternoon at a musical soirée, where the ladies of the court tutted and clucked behind their fans, and ventured looks at their monarch that were as greedy as they were pitying. It was the same at the whist game before supper. In the Mirror Gallery, cold and bright as the heart of an iceberg, the shuffle of cards was interspersed with all manner of sly whispering.

'Vultures!' Eleri spat, as soon as she and Pattern were alone. 'How they long to pick over my poor dead bones! I am tempted to drive away so far and so fast tomorrow that no one will catch me or see me ever again.'

Perhaps the same notion had occurred to Prince Leopold, for he appointed as her chaperone the most senior and least agreeable of her ladies-in-waiting. Lady Agatha Craddock was an iron-grey woman with an iron-grey manner, who made no attempt to hide her displeasure at having been assigned to such a tedious task.

They departed just after dawn in the unmarked carriage that royalty used when travelling on private business. Lady Agatha's displeasure only increased when, two hours into the journey, they stopped to change horses at a coaching inn. 'Surely the von Bliven estate lies to the west of here?' she remarked, frowning at the window as they set off again upon the road.

'Yes,' said Eleri airily, 'but I have decided I don't wish to go there after all. The castle's situation is famously damp, and I have a ticklish sort of throat this morning.' She coughed for effect. 'What's more, I remember my dear godmama always spoke very warmly of the mineral spring at Llanotto Wells. I am sure that taking the waters there will do me a power of good.'

'Llanotto Wells! Llanotto *Wells*? Really, Your Highness, I must protest. This is most irregular. It is not at all what I or your uncle were led to believe—'

'It does not matter what you or he believe about

anything,' Eleri retorted. 'I may not be of age, but I am still Head of State, and I shall visit whichever part of my Duchy I choose.' She settled herself more comfortably upon the seat. 'You look peaky, Craddock. Perhaps you would benefit from taking the waters too. It might put some colour in your cheeks.'

Their coachman and co-conspirator was Franz, Dilys's particular friend. The story Pattern gave was that the Grand Duchess wished to visit an old servant of her father's of whom Prince Leopold did not approve. Although Dilys – flattered by this sign of Royal Favour, and anxious to prove her helpfulness – had urged Franz to accept the commission, he still took some persuading. He had weighed the fat pouch of coins the Grand Duchess had pressed on him and frowned.

'But Your Highness, if Prince Leopold were to find out my part in this—'

'He won't,' Eleri had said firmly. 'And if you are questioned, you will simply tell him you were following orders, and that however much you protested, I would not be denied.' Her eyes widened in appeal. 'Did you never play truant when you were a little boy?'

At this, Franz had grinned, so his dimples danced. Pattern saw why Dilys was so fond of him.

And so it was they travelled the remaining fifteen miles to where the town of Llanotto Wells perched high on the hills above the Forest of Annwn. This was not a high-society resort like the town of Brecon-Baden, with its horse-racing track and theatres and famous Pump Room. It was mostly frequented by the elderly and unfashionable, who were not in a position to mind that the baths were cold rather than hot, or that the mineral water had the distinct flavour of mud.

They drew up to the so-called Royal Hotel, a dark and musty establishment furnished with a great quantity of chintz. Pattern went within to enquire about taking a suite. She represented herself as maid to Lady Agatha, who was bringing her invalid niece to take the waters. The concierge was so busy bowing and scraping as he showed them to their rooms that he barely glanced at the Grand Duchess, who was swaddled up to her ears in an invalid's muffler and scarf.

Lady Agatha surveyed their quarters with iron-grey disdain. 'Small wonder you wish your visit to this fleapit to be incognito, Your Highness. What do you propose first? Are we to wash in the local slime-bath, or merely drink from it?'

'I propose,' said Eleri brightly, 'a nice cup of tea, prepared in the nice English manner. Pattern is quite the Angel of the Brew.'

Pattern gave her a look. She thought Eleri's good cheer must appear highly suspicious. However, after a long and tiresome morning on the road, Lady Agatha was not disposed to turn away refreshment.

Almost with the first sip from the cup that Pattern gave her, the woman began to nod. Her head drooped forward over table and cup – was resolutely jerked back, then drooped again. And again. Her eyes began to close. She blinked rapidly, took another sip of tea to keep herself awake . . . and continued sipping herself into sleep. Five minutes later, she was slumped and snoring in her chair.

After a somewhat breathless pause, Eleri tiptoed

over and tweaked her nose. There was no response.

'What in heaven did you give her?'

'It's a new sleeping tonic I've been working on,' Pattern replied with quiet pride. 'De Quincey's Cordial by way of Hargreave's Elixir of Lethe, with a few refinements of my own. By my calculations, she should be out for the afternoon.'

A note was left for Lady Agatha, in the event she woke up before they returned, to say that mistress and maid were touring the town and that they hoped she had a pleasant rest in the meantime. Franz was already settled in the stable block with a mug of ale. They were able to slip out of the hotel and into an empty outbuilding without trouble. Here Pattern changed into her plainest print dress, and helped Eleri pin up her hair under a peaked cap. The Grand Duchess was disguised in a costume of boy's breeches, shirt and jacket that Pattern had purloined from the castle laundries. Both were equipped with stout shoes and walking sticks for their walk into the forest; Pattern carried a spy-glass.

The town did not improve on closer acquaintance. The only people out in it were the elderly and infirm. The gaily painted villas had faded to shabby pastel hues, the flowers drooped in their hanging baskets, and smoke belched from a giant bottle-shaped brick building on the riverbank below.

'It's the kiln of a porcelain manufactory,' Eleri said, putting the spy-glass to her eye. 'I wonder that it is here at all, for most of our potteries are in the east of the Duchy. I have to tour there once a year to bill and coo over their mouldy old plates.'

Pattern wondered about it too. She took out their map of paths through the forest, and looked out at the undulating mass of trees spread out over the valley. Summer was over, and the leaves glimmered with copper and bronze. Somewhere in their depths was the Prince's hunting lodge. But her eye kept being drawn back to the bottle kiln.

A little way along, they came upon a grocer's, and went inside to purchase food for their expedition. After exchanging pleasantries with the grandmotherly shopkeeper, Pattern ventured a question.

'The manufactory down by the river . . . it looks to be a recent construction?'

'Oh yes, it has only been put up this last year. But if you and your brother are looking for work, I fear you are out of luck. The owner is a foreigner, and so are his labourers – Orientals of some kind, I believe. They live on site and are hardly ever seen outside it, for they don't speak English, let alone the Elffish tongue. We have a delivery made up for them this afternoon, but it will be their driver who comes and collects it, and he has barely spoken more than two or three words to us in all this time.'

'Surely a foreign owner would need a special licence from the Grand Duchess?' Eleri piped up.

'They have a Royal Warrant from Prince Leopold, and I'm sure that's much the same thing.'

'Leopold! Ha! I should have—'

Pattern nudged Eleri sharply in the ribs. However, the shopkeeper was rambling on, oblivious. The Prince was such an affable gentleman, and often passed

through town on his way to his hunting lodge. Only last winter he had come and taken tea at the Royal Hotel and opened the Christmas bazaar. 'Folk were alarmed when construction of the pottery began, especially when we learned there would be no jobs. And we worried about the effect of the smoke, you know, on the health and peace of our visitors. But the Prince has settled everything with the pottery's owner. He is going to use the taxes raised from the manufactory to quite overhaul the town. For he said, with only a little investment, we could become as fashionable as Brecon-Baden. And why not indeed? Our waters are as healthful; our situation quite as picturesque. Yes, there are great plans afoot for Llanotto Wells. Come back in a year and I'm sure you will not recognize us.' Then she lowered her voice. 'Always supposing, of course, that Elffinberg's *present troubles* are resolved.'

Eleri was plucking at Pattern's sleeve. As soon as they were out of the shop, she burst out. 'We can forget the hunting lodge! Don't you see? The pottery is my uncle's. He will be putting the stolen children to work there. It is the perfect place to hide them, and turn a profit on their labours too.'

She explained that her father the Grand Duke had passed several laws to improve the pay and conditions in the potteries, and it was now illegal for them to employ children of under thirteen years of age. Formerly, a great many used to sicken from Potter's Rot, a disease of the lungs that children are especially vulnerable to. 'Poor mites! I myself will break open their prison. Imagine it, Pattern: everyone will hail me as a great saviour, while my uncle will be utterly disgraced. I'll put him on trial for high treason and kidnapping and breaking the labour laws!'

'But however are we to get inside? The shopkeeper said hardly anyone goes in or out.'

'Except for the delivery cart, remember. Don't you see? We can build our very own Trojan horse out of their groceries.'

Eleri hurried round to the yard at the back of the shop. Pattern followed more slowly. Sure enough, when they peeked over the wall, they saw a young

fellow engaged in loading a covered wagon with canned goods, sides of bacon and other household items.

'Everything is falling exactly into place,' Eleri crowed. 'This is more than blind luck. It is a sign that my fortunes are on the turn at last.'

The man disappeared into the shop to fetch his next load. Before Pattern could stop her, Eleri darted into the yard and hopped into the back of the wagon. She beckoned to Pattern to follow. Pattern shook her head and gestured to Eleri to get out. Eleri scowled

and beckoned again, with even more emphasis. And so Pattern, who had not quite got out of the habit of doing as she was told, went to join the Grand Duchess in her hiding place between bags of potatoes and onions, with only bit of sacking to pull over their heads.

'I do not think this is at all sensible,' she whispered. 'Even if we are not discovered and gain entrance to the place, we will then be trapped inside without any means of protection or escape.'

'Well, *I* think it is an excellent plan, and you are peevish because you did not come up with it yourself,' Eleri hissed back. 'As for our defence, I am one step ahead of you there too. Look!' She opened her jacket to reveal the handle of a pistol stowed in her belt. 'It was my papa's and he showed me how to use it. Like him, I am sure to be an exceedingly good shot.'

Pattern's alarm only increased. But before she could make any further protest, they heard someone else come into the yard and speak a few halting, heavily accented words to the shopworker. There was a brief discussion of payment, as a couple of sacks were opened

and inspected. Pattern hardly dared breathe while this was going on; Eleri's hand closed round hers in a sweaty grip. Yet they remained undetected. Minutes later, the canvas covering was tied in place, the wagon lurched forward, and they were rattling out of town along the road that wound down to the river.

CHAPTER FIFTEEN

❧ ❧

Dishonesty seldom fails to be detected.

J. Bulcock, *The Duties of a Lady's Maid*

❧ ❧

Eleri's plan, such as it was, began well. After a most uncomfortable twenty minutes jolting among the potatoes, they heard the sounds of doors or gates opening and of the pony clattering across a cobbled yard full of movement and noise. Then the wagon turned a corner, and the noise faded away.

All too soon, someone fumbled at the ties closing the canvas cover. A Chinese face peered in.

'Stand and deliver!'

The Grand Duchess shot up from amidst the groceries, her pistol aimed squarely at the man's forehead.

Her target seemed more perplexed than alarmed. He looked about him, baffled and blinking, as Eleri scrambled out from the wagon, managing to keep her aim steady all the time.

'Put up your hands! Up – like this! Up!'

Slowly, the Chinese gentleman did as he was asked, still with an air of polite puzzlement.

They were in a kind of alley between the outer wall of the manufactory and a storage facility. Its doors were open for the delivery, a wheeled trolley standing by. Nobody else was in view.

'Pattern, secure the prisoner. You'd best gag him too.'

'I'm very sorry, sir,' Pattern murmured, fixing a length of torn canvas round the man's mouth and checking that his hands were securely fastened behind his back with layers of string from the food sacks. She finished off both knots with a neatly looped bow. 'I trust you will not be inconvenienced for long.'

It would be rude to stare, but Pattern had never seen someone from China before, except on a London theatre bill promoting the magical feats of a Mr Foo Ping-Ting, 'Imperial Enchanter of the Orient'. This man looked disappointingly ordinary. He did not have a pigtail, or flowing silk robes and a pointy hat, and was dressed the same as any manufactory worker.

His eyes darted towards the alleyway, where the pony waited by the wagon. Perhaps he was expecting someone. In any case, it could not be long before they were interrupted. Pattern felt all the precariousness of their position, and all the frustration of having been dragged into this madcap scheme against her will.

For Eleri, however, there were no misgivings. Everything was proceeding exactly as she had hoped. 'Let us survey the enemy terrain!'

The larder was one of a series of storage rooms. Prodding their captive with her pistol, Eleri herded him past sacks of salt and sand and other materials

necessary for the manufacture of clay, through to the sturdy metal door at the end of the building. Unlike the others, it was locked. 'And what have we here? A punishment cell, perhaps.' She jangled the set of keys she had taken from the prisoner's waist. 'Which one?' she demanded.

Her expression was so exceedingly fierce the man did not hesitate long before waggling his eyebrows to indicate the correct key. In truth, Pattern expected to find nothing more remarkable than another supply cupboard. Yet the door opened on a small workroom stacked with wooden kegs and cases marked with Chinese characters. The shelves held slabs of slate and shallow earthenware dishes, and there was a bench set up with a mortar and pestle. Leather buckets filled with sand hung from hooks in the wall. There was a distinct whiff of rotten eggs – the sulphurous smell Pattern remembered from the crater at Caer Grunwald.

'I don't know for sure,' she said, swallowing hard, 'but it is very possible those kegs contain explosives. It is really not safe for us to be here. You must

come back with a search warrant and armed men, and all the proper authorities.'

'Yes, but what of the children?' said Eleri impatiently. 'We cannot leave before we have some sight of them.' She closed the door on the kegs and marched their captive back the way they had come, to the small window in the larder. Outside, more Chinese men hurried back and forth loading and unloading

clay into the kiln. The flaming oven mouth put Pattern uncomfortably in mind of the dragon; the men closest to them had scorched red faces from the heat.

Eleri put the spy-glass to her eye, examining the cluster of red-brick warehouses and workshops beyond the kiln yard. 'The children will be in the dipping house, I expect,' she said. 'Since the fumes from the lead-glaze are very noxious, skilled workers avoid it. Or else they will be employed as pattern-cutters. Their fingers are small, and so especially nimble with the scissors.'

Pattern felt a rising twitch of exasperation. 'Wherever they are kept, they will be locked up and under guard.'

'No matter. *We* have a hostage. If he will not tell us where the children are himself, we will parade him at the point of my gun and demand to be taken to them.'

'What d'you think you're doing? This isn't a holiday camp! Get back to work!'

It was a very large and angry Elffishman, wearing a foreman's coat. Then he looked at them more closely. 'Wait a minute – you don't belong here. Who the hell are you, and how the blazes did you get in?'

Eleri immediately pulled the prisoner in front of her and Pattern. 'Stay back or I shoot!'

But the foreman merely guffawed. 'Go ahead. He's only the quartermaster; we can easily find another one.'

Eleri dug the pistol into the unfortunate quartermaster's side, causing him to yelp, but her discomfiture was clear. The foreman advanced upon them, swinging a truncheon in his hands. His meaty red face was shiny with satisfaction.

'Trespass is a criminal offence, my lad, and industrial espionage is more serious still. Or maybe you and your friend only meant to go as far as armed robbery. Either way, you're in a world of trouble . . .'

Pattern seized the handle of a loading-trolley and charged, running it into the foreman's knees as hard and fast as she was able. Taken by surprise, the man stumbled, and almost fell.

'Run!' she shouted.

Both girls pelted out into the alley. It led straight into the hot and smoky kiln yard. They skidded across the cobbles, tripping over wheelbarrows and workers

alike, as the foreman charged after them.

'Stop! There's no way out; the gates are locked.'

'*You're* the one who's trapped,' Eleri retorted. 'You won't escape justice. I'm your Grand Duchess; no one can touch me!'

It was perhaps just as well her boast was lost in the general uproar.

She and Pattern bolted through the nearest doorway into a room full of churning vats of sloppy liquid clay and another clanking with mechanical presses, then through a workshop crammed with men hunched over potter's wheels. It was there they nearly ran right into a couple of ragged little boys staggering under the weight of heavy plaster moulds. Their faces were wan and thin; their eyes red.

'You were right!' Pattern gasped. 'And look – up there!'

Another small blond head peeped from behind a barred window in the courtyard outside. But there was no time to stop; no time to question. All their energies had to be focused on their own escape, as they fled through a mazy complex of high brick buildings, their view obscured and breath choked by the clouds of clay dust that hung thickly in the air. An alarm bell began to clang. The foreman was joined by two Chinese guards.

Turning another corner brought them face to face with an office marked 'Management', from which another Elffishman suddenly appeared. He was small and dapper, with a pointed black beard. 'What is the meaning of this ballyhoo?'

'Out of my way!' screamed Eleri, brandishing her pistol as she pushed him aside. Pulling Pattern along behind her, she charged through another set of doors into a warehouse filled with towering racks of ceramics ready for market. Packing crates spilling over with straw lined the aisles. This time, however, there was no exit. They were trapped.

The meaty foreman advanced, grinning, flanked by the two guards.

'Come quietly, now, and we'll try not to break too many bones.'

'Any damage must be paid for!' spluttered the

bearded gentleman, who was bringing up the rear.

But Eleri was not done. She had the light of battle in her eyes. Flushed and panting, she grabbed the nearest item to hand – an ornate black stoneware urn in the Roman style – and hurled it to the ground. The crash echoed through the warehouse.

The bearded gentleman shook his fist. 'These are precious artworks, you barbarian!'

Eleri laughed giddily. 'Not any more!' Next, she reached for a floral serving dish as wide as a carriage wheel and flung it at their pursuers, who were forced to duck for cover as it shattered into razor-sharp splinters. With Pattern scrambling to keep up, she ran off down the aisles, smashing and crashing and crushing as she went. Pitchers and platters, tureens and teapots – all reduced to smithereens. It made for an unholy din.

'STOP THAT MANIAC,' howled the bearded gentleman. 'Whatever it takes!'

That was when the foreman got out his own gun.

Pattern plucked at the tails of Eleri's jacket. 'You have to stop; please stop. He's going to shoot!'

But Eleri did not seem to hear. She rampaged on, a girl possessed. She turned down another aisle and started back towards their pursuers, turning whole dinner services into a storm of missiles.

'Wait, you don't understand,' Pattern pleaded with them. 'She's the Gr—'

It was no good. Before Pattern's horrified eyes, the foreman raised his pistol and took aim.

'No!'

A man emerged as if from nowhere, sprinting forward and slamming into Eleri so that she was knocked sideways into the wall. The bullet whistled past, grazing him on the shoulder.

'God's pocket, that was close,' he observed, with only a slight shake in his voice.

It was Madoc.

Chapter Sixteen

Nothing is more endearing than a frank confession.

J. Bulcock, *The Duties of a Lady's Maid*

'Bring me the fetters,' Madoc ordered. 'But stay back, all of you. I will deal with this.'

He was only a valet, yet here in his master's manufactory, he had a new kind of authority. The foreman and bearded manager made loud objections, but did as he asked.

'Trust me, and I will get you out of here, Your Highness,' he said, very softly, as he clipped the manacles around Pattern and Eleri's wrists.

All the fight had gone out of the Grand Duchess, although thanks to Pattern's expert pinning, her long hair remained hidden inside her cap, and her disguise, such as it was, seemed intact. She made only the faintest of protests.

With the intruders under lock and key, and the chains of their cuffs in his hands, Madoc turned back to his colleagues. 'My master will wish to handle this in person. I will take these miscreants to him directly, so that he can deal with them as he sees fit.'

'I really cannot see how . . .' spluttered the bearded gentleman.

'How your security was so easily breached by a couple of ragamuffins? That is a very good question.' Madoc examined his torn jacket, and his fingers came away smeared with blood. He looked at it distastefully. Otherwise, he was as neat as ever, gleaming pale hair lying smooth against his head. 'I'm sure my master will be most eager to hear your explanation for such a grievous blunder. I suggest you return to your office and

set about constructing a full report.' He looked round the scene of destruction with a weary eye. 'And get this mess cleared up. We will need an inventory of the day's losses.'

It all happened very quickly. Madoc hustled his two captives through the manufactory and out of the gates, straight into a waiting carriage. He directed the coachman to take them along the road into the cover of the forest, where it drew up in a secluded spot. They scarcely dared breathe until the manufactory was behind them, and Madoc undid the cuffs.

'Forgive me, Your Highness. I had to make the pretence convincing.' He paused. 'But your own pretence was a far riskier one. Didn't you realize how much danger you were in, alone and unprotected in such a place?'

'I know.' Eleri hung her head. 'It was very foolish. Pattern did not approve either, and I would not listen to her. But I was tired of sitting helplessly about, waiting for my fate to be decided. And then in that warehouse, surrounded by all those costly, fragile, pointless things . . . I don't know what came over me. But if it was to be my last act on earth, I was determined to enjoy it. And oh! It did feel good.'

'I see.' Madoc turned to Pattern with a quizzical arch of his brow. 'Well now, Miss Pattern, how is your reading getting along? Perhaps you are beginning to acquire a taste for fairy tales. Perhaps you take a new interest in their wicked uncles and captive princesses, and monsters that lurk in the dark.'

Pattern kept her tone level. 'If Prince Leopold is so wicked, then why are you working for him?'

'Yes,' said Eleri, sitting up straighter. 'I thought you were as black-hearted as he, but here you are, risking your own life to save mine. I do not understand it at all.'

'I don't entirely understand it myself.' Madoc suddenly looked very tired. 'It is true I am not a particularly good man, and working for the Prince has made me a worse one. I suppose I fell into the mire by degrees – as, perhaps, did he. One small mischief led to a bigger one, until we were both so far gone in wickedness there seemed no way back.' He sighed,

and his eyes closed briefly. 'So now I must make my confession. I visited the manufactory on my master's orders, to pass on his instructions and oversee the accounts. But my plan was to travel on, all the way to the border. I mean to flee the Duchy this night, and never come back.'

They stared at him.

'I have forged papers, under a new name. The coachman is in my pay. My worldly goods, such as they are, are stowed in this carriage. They include various small but costly trinkets stolen from my master the Prince. So you see I am not just a criminal servant, but a treacherous one.'

'Cowardly too,' Pattern said tartly. 'Whatever mess you find yourself in, you leave a far worse one for the rest of us.' It was hard to believe she had once been in awe of the man. He had always seemed so upright and sure-footed. But now he wore a rumpled, defeated look.

Eleri leaned forwards and grasped his hand. 'Madoc, you must know you cannot leave the country now. You must stay and redeem yourself. Whatever your former crimes, all will be pardoned – I give you my solemn word. We cannot let those poor children remain slaves to that foul manufactory. We cannot let my uncle win. At the very least, you owe it to me to tell all you know of his schemes.'

And so he did. Most of it was as they had already guessed, but he was able to supply some important details.

'The Prince knew that if Elffinberg was to believe the dragon had returned, a trail of destruction would not be enough. People would need to think they had seen the monster with their own eyes. He had already been in talks with a Chinese agent as part of plans to expand his porcelain business. The Chinese are, of course, famed for the excellence of their ceramics. But they are equally renowned for their skill with pyrotechnics, and it was this that inspired the Prince to conjure a dragon out of fire and smoke.

'Putting the stolen children to work in his pottery enabled him to solve two problems at a single stroke –

how to dispose of the dragon's so-called victims, and how to reduce his labour costs. All the adult workers are Chinese, recruited from the Emperor's own porcelain manufactory at some expense. For the Prince could not rely on local craftsmen to keep his secret safe.'

'It's not only pots he's storing there. We saw a cache of explosives too,' said Pattern.

Madoc smiled. 'The Chinese made gunpowder when our ancestors were living half-naked in mud huts. Pyrotechnics is both a science and an art, and one that can be employed to terrifying effect – especially on simple folk who are already in fear of their lives.'

'They aren't the only ones,' said Eleri with feeling.

'Believe me, Your Highness, you have never been in danger of your life. Your uncle is many things, but he is not a murderer.'

'So how does he intend for his firework dragon to dispose of me?'

'There is a private sanatorium in Switzerland,' Madoc answered reluctantly. 'A small and closely guarded establishment for those suffering from diseases of the brain. He means to spirit you away and keep you there, disguised as the daughter of a wealthy English industrialist: an English girl who is under the delusion she is Elffish royalty.'

'Imprisoned in such a place, it would not take long for true lunacy to take hold.' Eleri shuddered. 'I believe I would almost prefer to be fed to a dragon.'

An uncomfortable silence fell in the carriage. Madoc cleared his throat.

'I know I can never atone for my part in this, Your Highness. It is only right that I carry the shame of it now and for always. But if you will permit me to make a suggestion . . . ?'

Eleri indicated that he should.

'The Prince Elffin's Day Ball is but three days away. All the great and good of the Duchy will be in attendance. It is customary for the Grand Duchess to address her guests, paying tribute to the assembled company and the glory of the nation.'

'Yes, I have to make the same sort of speech every year, and very tedious it is.'

'It is also the perfect opportunity to denounce your uncle: in public, surrounded by people of consequence. He would not dare attack you in such a setting, and your audience will be bound to listen.'

'An ambush!' Eleri visibly brightened.

'Her Highness would need proof,' Pattern cautioned. 'No doubt the Prince's henchmen at the pottery are already preparing to hide the captive children elsewhere and removing all trace of the explosives.'

'I will do my best to conceal your invasion of the manufactory from the Prince, and I can supply evidence too,' said Madoc. 'I will need a little time, that's all.' Like the Grand Duchess, he looked newly energized by the thought of action. 'The Prince and his accomplices often meet at the hunting lodge to refine their schemes. When he is at court, the place is all shut up, and patrolled by his private guard. But I am sent there sometimes on errands, and that is where I will search for evidence to build a case against him. I shall unearth his correspondence with the agent in China and the manager of the Swiss sanatorium. There will be receipts for the fireworks and payments to his foreign workers. And if you agree, I will send them to you by way of the coachman, Howell. He has as much reason to hate the Prince as anyone, for Leopold turned his parents out of their cottage to make way for the expansion of his estate, leaving them destitute.'

Light was fading by the time Eleri and Pattern parted from Madoc, and made their weary way back to Llanotto Wells. Once changed into their usual attire, they found Lady Agatha awake and alert, and pacing about in an angry manner. It was clear she suspected mischief of some kind, while having nothing certain to accuse them of, and being uncomfortably aware that she would look foolish at best and negligent at worst if the Prince were to find out her charge had escaped her. She vented her feelings in the guise of concern for the Grand Duchess's health. 'If you are suffering from a cough, Your Highness, you should not have stayed out so long. You could have caught a chill. Besides, these are strange and threatening times. Who knows what

other dangers you might have met with?'

Eleri was all innocence. 'Gracious, what a vivid imagination you have! You talk as if Llanotto Wells were a hotbed of radicals and revolutionaries.'

The journey back to the castle seemed to take much longer than the journey away from it. Pattern slipped into an uneasy doze. She dreamed of the dragon again, though this time it was swathed in billows of dirty smoke, from which a forked tongue flickered.

'Little girl, don't you wish to look into my heart of flame? My fires burn black and bright, and they are full of secrets. For I have many stories to tell – of the tears of princesses, the rage of warriors; the humbling of the mighty, and the despair of the brave . . .'

'Pattern!'

Pattern woke up with a start. Eleri was shaking her arm. 'Whatever are you babbling about?'

'I . . . I don't remember, Your Highness. It was a dream; I'm sorry.'

Blearily she turned to the window to mark their progress, when her eye was caught by a gush of reddish-black smoke on the horizon.

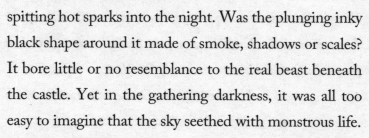

Lady Agatha and the Grand Duchess were soon as riveted by the sight as she. A distant coil of smoke curled and plunged with sinuous power, the sky around it suffused by a deep red glare. The scene was then illuminated by a furious streak of light, as a cascade of fire rumbled and cackled, spitting hot sparks into the night. Was the plunging inky black shape around it made of smoke, shadows or scales? It bore little or no resemblance to the real beast beneath the castle. Yet in the gathering darkness, it was all too easy to imagine that the sky seethed with monstrous life.

Franz lashed the horses, and the carriage rattled away with all speed from the sight. But shaken as she was, there was no mistaking Lady Agatha's smirk of satisfaction as she settled back in her seat.

'We cannot be too careful, Your Highness,' she said. 'A dark power is rising, and it has the House of Elffin in its sights.'

Chapter Seventeen

❧ ❧

You should endeavour to employ every minute in improving yourself in such things as you may be deficient in, and in practising what is not sufficiently familiar.

J. Bulcock, *The Duties of a Lady's Maid*

❧ ❧

In different circumstances, Pattern might have enjoyed the preparations for the Prince Elffin's Day Ball. The entire social world of the Grand Duchy was invited, making even the State Banquet seem a small, casual affair. The provision of a buffet supper pushed the castle kitchens to their limit, and taxed the resources of all the local pastry-cooks and confectioners. The two fashionable hairdressers in town were engaged six-deep, and on the night itself no carriage was to be had for love or money at the posting establishments.

There was even a new sense of purposefulness to the scurrying masses below stairs. As time wore on, their efforts became progressively more clumsy and cantankerous, but Pattern would never have guessed so much activity could be wrung from so inefficient a household.

Fairy lights were strung up around the central courtyard and along the length of the great avenue. An army of groundsmen appeared as if from nowhere to weed, sweep and clip their way across the terraces and lawns. Inside, dust stirred up by long-overdue sweeping and polishing made the elderly courtiers totter and sneeze. The castle's halls took on a surface brightness that did much to dispel the air of anxious gloom that had lately settled on the place.

And Prince Leopold, it seemed, was everywhere. In the kitchens – enquiring as to the seasoning of a

syllabub. By the grand fountain – pointing out a missing bulb on a string of lights. In the Musicians' Gallery – debating the merits of the *Danse Ecossoise* versus the *Danse Espagnuole*. His cheeks were rosier than ever, his golden curls had acquired an extra bounce. He had a suggestion for everything; a compliment and kindly twinkle for all. 'Miss Pattern! You look as if the cares of the world are on your shoulders. Don't you approve of parties? For there is music in your heart – I am sure of it. Dreams of music and dancing, and the sparkle of champagne! I hope your mistress will save you a bonbon or two at the very least.'

'Thank you, Your Highness, but I do not care for them.'

He thinks me a child, thought Pattern, whose favours can be bought with spun sugar. But then he probably believes that everyone has a price.

'My uncle has called an extraordinary meeting of the Council of State for the day after the ball,' Eleri told her that afternoon. 'It's meant to be a secret, yet everyone knows the Council will be debating the dragon. When they are all tired and hoarse from talking, that is when

Leopold will strike. It won't be him but one of his cronies who will first propose my sacrifice. No doubt he'll put on a great show of reluctance, and weep all manner of crocodile tears. But the motion will be carried, make no mistake. Then it will go before parliament, and all will be lost.'

They had gone to the chapel again, at Pattern's urging, since she wanted to examine the wall paintings. She did not know what she was looking for, exactly; only that they were in need of whatever guidance they could find. She looked especially closely at the picture of Prince Elffin kneeling by the fire, surrounded by various strange objects.

'What do you think this is about?'

'It could be a scene of old magic, to show how the Prince first tamed the dragon,' Eleri replied. 'Or the images are merely allegorical – to be symbols of his character and deeds, you know, rather than actual events.' She ran a finger along the part of the wall that concealed the passage to the dragon's lair. 'But for so long as the dragon sleeps, it is my uncle who is the enemy. We cannot fight *him* with magic, much as I would like to turn him into a cross-eyed toad.'

This was certainly true. Yet the Grand Duchess's sleep-talking, and her own disturbed dreams, made Pattern question how deeply the dragon slumbered. Her candle flickered in the draught so that light danced on the fresco's flaking colours and crude lines, giving them an eerie illusion of life. She was not sorry to shut the chapel door behind them.

Their only real source of news was the *Elffish Enquirer* – which still preferred to trade in hints and allusions – and Dilys, who proved a somewhat reluctant informant. Dilys was much troubled by what Franz had reported of his trip to Llanotto, and it was clear the girl did not quite know what to make of the Grand Duchess's position, or how Pattern had become so closely involved in her affairs.

Ever since Pattern's visit to Caer Grunwald, a crowd of protesters gathered daily outside the castle gates. Many of the missing children's relatives kept vigil there, sombre faced and dressed in black. Another crowd was encamped outside the parliament building. The approaching ball roused both groups to new heights of indignation. Shame on the court for making merry at such a time! What was the Grand Duchess thinking?

In fact, it was a matter of constant speculation among commoners and nobility alike as to how much the Grand Duchess knew about the threat to Elffinberg. Did she understand her duty? Was she ready to fulfil it? Surely her dear uncle would try to prepare her for all eventualities. Or would he shield her from the evil as best he could, right up to the last possible moment?

*

In the midst of all this conjecture and confusion, Eleri and Pattern's principal consolation was that Madoc had proved good as his word. Howell, the coachman, had already made his first visit to the castle, delivering a packet of documents hidden within a hatbox. A heavyset, unsmiling man, he promised a second delivery on the morning of the ball. They were particularly anxious to know the fate of the children trapped in the manufactory, and what new prison they might have been transferred to.

As a distraction, Eleri poured her energies into crafting the speech she would make to denounce her uncle. Her eyes flashed and colour rose as she strode about her chamber, flinging out her arms one moment, beating her breast the next, as she worked her way through a crescendo of accusations.

'I think,' Pattern counselled, after a decent pause, 'that perhaps it would be better to keep your natural emotions in check. You must not only make the case against your uncle, but demonstrate your own statesmanship. It's right that you are angry, but you must be the voice of reason above all else.'

Many more drafts were written, many more recitals given, until Eleri's speech was dispassionate, logical and remorseless enough to satisfy both. Eleri called Pattern a tyrant and a slave-driver, but allowed the final version was much improved on her first attempt.

When not engaged in speechifying, Eleri's principal occupation was looking over the invitation list to identify potential allies and enemies in the guests. Prince Leopold had recruited people from all levels of society to his plot, from his personal guard to the foreman and manager of his pottery, to venerable nobles in the Council of State. They too would have to be flushed out, made to bear witness, and punished accordingly.

'I see the Ap Erwin clan are attending. They are my nearest relations, and so the eldest daughter, Cousin Hilde, is next in line to be dragon-fodder. I'd feel sorry for her, if she were not a selfish brat who cut off the tail on my rocking-horse . . . Who knows where Lord and Lady Prosser's loyalties lie, but they're so stupid it

hardly matters. I dined with them the other day, and Lady P thought the Danube was a city in France! . . . Ha! No surprise to find the Marquis of Neu-Harlech on the list. He goes hunting with Leopold, and is one of his biggest bootlickers on the Council . . . And here we have the Honourable Ludwig Jones. His parents have planned for us to wed since we were both in our cradles. *They*, at least, will not wish me dead . . .'

Pattern watched Eleri pore over the list. The girl was full of restless energy, but her eyes were shadowed, and her fingernails bitten to the quick. She herself had not dreamed of the dragon again, but she feared it haunted Eleri's sleep. On two occasions she had gone to check on the Grand Duchess after she had gone to bed, and heard the girl pleading in her sleep, then give voice to strange chuckles and rasping hisses that seemed to have no human source. It sickened Pattern to hear them, and for long afterwards dread moved through her like infected blood. Yet in the morning, the Grand Duchess had no memory of anything untoward.

CHAPTER EIGHTEEN

It is in parties of pleasure, and at places of public amusement, that familiarity is most contagious, and may be to you most dangerous.

J. Bulcock, *The Duties of a Lady's Maid*

The day of the ball was unusually hot. It had been a very dry summer, and though it was only October, the parched trees had already begun to drop their leaves, and the lawns were patched with brown. Returning from an errand in town, Pattern viewed the castle through a blurry haze of heat, and was put in mind

of a vast sweating hulk of yellowish cheese. A fug of perspiration settled below stairs to join the steam and smells from the kitchen, and even the lords and ladies suffered from a creeping moisture about their person that no amount of iced refreshment or fan-wafting could dispel. There was not so much as the hint of a breeze. The whole country seemed to be holding its breath.

For those attending the ball, preparations began mid-afternoon. After reclining in a warm bath, the Grand Duchess took a quick dip in a cold one to polish her skin. Her nails were trimmed, and her complexion anointed with every potion and powder at Pattern's disposal. Her hair was braided, combed, coaxed and curled. Both girls were nervous, and Pattern, normally so deft and sure, stumbled more than once in her wielding of the pins.

She was just readjusting a tendril of curl to her satisfaction when two maids shuffled into the chamber, bearing a large box done up in velvet ribbons. 'A present from Prince Leopold, Your Highness.'

'What do you think it is?' Eleri asked after they had gone. 'Poisoned chocolates? A keg of gunpowder?'

Pattern lifted out a sumptuous white ball gown, its bodice sewn all over with crystals and pearls. Eleri gingerly poked the sleeves. 'Hmph. It still might be booby-trapped.'

'Well, there are no spikes sewn into the hems that I can see. It is probably best you wear it. You don't want to raise your uncle's suspicions at so late an hour. And it *is* very fine.'

Eleri had planned to wear a gown of deep rose satin, made up according to the latest Parisian style, but the fabric was heavier and would be much less comfortable in the heat of a crowded ballroom. Pattern could find no fault with the measurements of Prince Leopold's gift, for it fitted Eleri like a glove. They had already selected the simplest tiara in the Crown Jewel collection: a delicate filigree of diamonds and white gold.

Tiara in place, Eleri stood before the looking-glass. 'I have to allow the man has better taste in frocks than he does in porcelain. What do you think, Pattern? Am

I grown beautiful, like my mama? Am I a picture-book princess?'

'I think . . . you look a real heroine, not a fairy-tale one.'

'What does that mean?'

Pattern considered. She had come to realize that a person did not have to be picturesque to be worthy of adventure. Everyone was the hero of their own story. But true heroism, surely, was the part you played in the story of others. 'It means I think you look like a leader.'

'Then I will try to act like one.' Eleri straightened her shoulders. 'Is everything ready?'

'It is.'

Thanks to Madoc, they had assembled quite a collection of invoices and receipts, lists of names and materials, maps and diagrams. Some of the information was easy to decipher; other documents would need longer study for their import to be understood. Pattern had taken the most-incriminating papers, folded them up very small, and hidden them in the lining of her sewing basket. During their conference in the forest,

Madoc had revealed the existence of several spy-holes cut in the walls between the servants' rat-runs and the main castle. One of them overlooked the ballroom, and it was here Pattern would position herself, ready for Eleri to give the cue. Then she would step out and present the papers to her mistress.

Traditionally, the Grand Duchess addressed her guests at midnight, just before the buffet. It was now eight. The fairy lights twinkled in the pine trees, the flaming cressets to either side of the portico spat sparks into the evening air. The candles were lit and champagne was chilled. The castle was ready, and so were they.

Pattern went first. On her way out of the room, Eleri caught her by the hand. 'You are my only friend, Pattern, but I couldn't hope for a better one.' She bit her lip. 'I have decided that perhaps the reason my people are so afraid – so credulous and cowed – is because I, their Grand Duchess, am no better. I have allowed myself to be angry and frightened for too long. But you make me brave. I think if I can become worthy of your friendship, then maybe I will be worth

something to my country too.'

Tears prickled in Pattern's eyes. She longed to make a reply as heartfelt as it was eloquent. But friendship was still a new language to her, and her stumbled tongue could not find the words. She took refuge in a curtsy and smile.

Despite the momentous events that loomed ahead, Pattern was not entirely untouched by the excitement of the occasion. She paused a moment by the window of the upper gallery as the first carriages drew up outside and disgorged their plumed and puffed-up cargo.

'And so the circus begins.'

Madoc had performed his usual trick of appearing out of thin air. Pattern was relieved to see him. She had not laid eyes on the valet since leaving Llanotto Wells. He looked strained, however, and his complexion was an unhealthy grey. Life as a double agent was clearly taking its toll. Perhaps this accounted for his acid tone.

'Look at them! So much wealth and privilege, so much education and refinement! Yet hardly an original thought or useful skill between them.'

'Would we be any better if we had been born to their position?'

'I believe *you* would, Miss Pattern. Some people will always want to make the best of themselves, and what they see around them. But a life of ease is an enemy to enterprise. There may come a time when our masters will discover for themselves just how hapless they are beneath their gilding.' He shook his head, and his smile shimmered. 'Birth is an accident. Luck, however, is something we can make for ourselves. And heaven knows, Miss Pattern, we are in need of it tonight.'

The valet moved on before she could respond. Pattern was never quite sure of what to say to Madoc, in any case. Hugging her sewing basket to her chest, she prepared to take up her position. The back stairs reverberated to the sound of hurrying feet, laboured breath and muttered curses, as people elbowed their way past each other on an endless round of chores. History did not relate who had made the spy-holes, and Pattern did not know how many of the servantry

knew their secret. The one she was using had been most cunningly concealed, and was in the back of a small store whose wall overlooked the ballroom. Madoc – via Howell, the coachman – had supplied her with a key to lock it from the inside, and although the space was cramped and cluttered, she had found time earlier in the day to furnish it with a stool.

Her first squint through the spy-hole half blinded her. Thousands of beeswax candles were reflected in the ballroom's mirrored walls. They swam in the floor's polished glimmer, glittered in the drops of the chandeliers, and sparkled in the jewels of the guests. No doubt Madoc was right, and most of these people amounted to very little if stripped of their costly embellishments. All the same, it made for a very splendid sight.

A trumpet fanfare sounded from the Musicians' Gallery high up under the roof. The buzzing, rustling crowd fell silent as the doors were flung wide by pages and, preceded by the Chamberlain, Her Royal Highness Arianwen Eleri Charlotte Louise, Grand Duchess

of Elffinberg,
made her Grand
Entrance to the
Prince Elffin's
Day Ball.

As one, the
assembly swayed into
curtsy and bow as
Eleri walked towards
the large gilded chair
on the crimson dais.
It was backed by
crimson draperies
and stood beneath a fringed canopy of the same colour.
A number of other spindly gold chairs were arranged
upon the wide platform, for the comfort of Prince
Leopold and other courtiers, who processed behind
their monarch.

Among the richly glowing fabrics, the simplicity
of Eleri's white dress marked her out even more than
the isolation of her rank. She looked very small and

pale and upright as she made her way across the room. Once she had taken her seat, the musicians struck up, and almost immediately afterwards she was on her feet again – a buck-toothed youth wearing a yellow sash had come to ask for her hand. Now she must open the ball by leading the first dance. Guests took their places for the quadrille.

Prince Leopold, usually a tireless dancer, did not participate. He slumped on the dais in near silence, frowning and picking his nails. After the rigours of the quadrille, a footman presented Eleri with a glass of lemonade but the Prince waved away all refreshment, and rebuffed all attempts at conversation.

Pattern regretted bringing no refreshment for herself. Hours passed, and she grew weary in her cupboard. Her legs were stiff, her back sore from hunching to look through the spy-hole. After a while, she even tired of casting a professional eye over the cut and cloth of the ladies' gowns, and the dressing of their hair. It must have been very warm, for the lily-white complexions got progressively redder, and a sheen of dampness was visible on even the finest brow. The dancing was as stiff as it was stately, and so was the talk. Nobody seemed truly at ease. This was more than the formality of the occasion or the closeness of the air. Everyone was thinking of the burnt fields, the lost children, the fires in the sky.

Yet Pattern was still unprepared when the castle's bell tolled midnight. It boomed over the song of the violins, the ripples of talk, and shuffle of slippered feet. As silence fell, Pattern felt her own body shiver like struck bronze.

Her mouth was dry and palms clammy as she freed the precious documents from their hiding place. She pressed her eye to the spy-hole to watch as Eleri rose from her chair, pausing only to take a cooling sip of lemonade. The crowd waited expectantly. Most had fixed their faces into expressions of polite appreciation. A few were already smothering yawns.

'Friends, countrymen. Honoured guests. On this our founding day, it is customary to speak of Elffinberg's glories. Now, however, is not the time. A grave danger menaces our land.'

A grave danger, but not the one you think, Pattern mouthed silently behind the panelling. She knew the speech as well as the Grand Duchess; both girls could have given it in their sleep. So why was Eleri slurring and stumbling over her words? And why had she paused? Had the heat of the room got too much for her?

'A grave danger . . . that is . . . not . . . but not what . . . not . . .'

The crowd shifted uneasily. Eleri's face was curiously slack, her eyes glazed. She seemed to sway.

'Not what I . . . you . . .'

An anxious murmuring swelled through the room.

Prince Leopold got to his feet and put a supportive arm around her shoulders.

'My dear niece is overcome by the emotion of the hour. We both hoped and prayed it would not come to this. But I must tell you that earlier today, Her Royal Highness summoned me to her chamber and said she had received the Sign.'

Gasps and sighs.

'Yes,' said the Prince, raising his voice, and lifting his chin in a tragical yet noble attitude. 'The voices of her ancestors have spoken to her. Elffin's Bane has demanded a blood ransom, and will not be denied. And so the Grand Duchess has decreed that tonight will be the night of her supreme sacrifice, for the continued peace and protection of our beloved land.'

As the room exploded into sobs of pity and cries of acclaim, all the breath was choked out of Pattern's body. Why didn't Eleri shout him down? Rage and resist? She just stood there, drooped, and blinked dully.

Pattern rose to her feet. She did not know what she was going to say or do once she got to the ballroom. She only knew she must act.

But the storeroom door opened even before she could put the key in the lock. A dark shape loomed over her; she caught the scent of aniseed . . . and an iron hand pressed a foul-smelling rag against her nose and mouth.

The world dissolved into blackness.

CHAPTER NINETEEN

⚭⚭ ⚭⚭

A sense of benefits received naturally inspires a grateful disposition, with a desire of making suitable returns.

J. Bulcock, *The Duties of a Lady's Maid*

⚭⚭ ⚭⚭

'Miss, Miss! Wake up!'

Pattern was assaulted by another odour, but this time she recognized the ammonia sharpness of sal volatile. Dilys had found the bottle of smelling salts in her pocket and was shoving it vigorously against Pattern's nostrils.

'Thank you . . . I am . . . I am recovered,' she managed

to say. She was slumped on a landing in the back stairs, and her head ached horribly. It took a moment for her to recollect what had brought her there. Her eyes widened in alarm as everything came rushing back, and she struggled to sit up. 'The Grand Duchess!'

'Hush now, and rest a while. You've had quite an ordeal.' Dilys's work-roughened hand patted hers. Franz the coachman regarded her anxiously from the corner. No one else could be seen in the dingy stairwell or passageway.

'How long have I been unconscious?'

'I don't rightly know,' Dilys replied. 'I fear it took a while for us to find you. I'd been coming up these stairs, you see, when I was nearly knocked off my feet by the Prince's valet. He had a more than usually shifty look about him and he rushed off without a word, your sewing basket under his arm. Very odd, it was. But the castle was in uproar after Prince Leopold and the Grand Duchess's announcement, and nobody knew which way was up . . . I thought that at such a time you would wish to be near to your mistress and that

p'raps you hadn't yet heard the news. So I went to your chamber and then hers to look for you. Then I came back down here and my eye was caught by that pearl brooch, the one Her Highness gave you, lying right outside the storeroom – here it is, look, though the pin is sadly bent. Well, I tried the door and found that it was locked, which it never was before, and I knew in my bones something was amiss. That's when I fetched Franz to break down the lock. Oh, we had such a fright when we saw you there, bound and gagged, and limp as the dead!'

Franz looked grim. 'You had a lucky escape. In all the confusion it could have been hours – days – before anyone found you.'

'I'm sure you're right. Thank you,' said Pattern distractedly. 'But tell me. Eleri – Her Highness – what –'

'It's a terrible business.' Dilys could not meet her eye. 'But if she's the only thing that stands between us and Elffin's Bane . . .'

'It is not what you think. The dragon does not . . .' Pattern paused. She had been about to say that it did not exist, but of course this was not true. 'The dragon attacks have been manufactured. By ordinary men, not monsters. It is a plot to usurp the Grand Duchess's throne, and I have the proof. At least . . . I did have it. Mr Madoc stole it from me, and imprisoned me in that cupboard to prevent me from exposing his master.'

Madoc had only ever pretended to betray Prince Leopold. When he recognized Pattern and Eleri in the pottery, and realized how much they must know, his agile mind had contrived a way of delaying them from further action, so that the Prince's ambush would take his victim entirely unawares. Something must have been slipped into the Grand Duchess's drink to numb her sensibilities; Pattern was not the only servant skilled in the use of such drugs. But she remained puzzled as to why Madoc had put himself between the Grand Duchess and the foreman's gun. Surely it would have been simpler for all concerned if Eleri had died by misadventure in the pottery? Could the Prince have another reason to continue with the dragon charade?

Pattern got to her feet. 'Where have they taken my mistress?'

'Up . . . up to the mountain,' Dilys faltered. 'Most everyone here has gone to escort her. Though she was close to fainting, she went quietly. Willingly, we thought . . . You might be able to see the last of the procession from the window.'

Pattern needed no more instruction. She rushed down towards the ballroom. The castle felt emptier than ever. There were no footmen idling by, no courtiers drifting through the echoing halls. Only the ticking of the clocks broke the silence. It was if the inhabitants had fled from some disaster: chairs were overturned, a tray of champagne saucers were scattered over the sodden carpet, a single dancing slipper lay, like Cinderella's, abandoned on the stairs.

In the white-panelled dining room, a feast was laid out for guests who would never come. The tables were wreathed in flowers and loaded with syllabubs, jellies and custards; turtle soup and oysters, gammon and roast veal. Sugar-paste sculptures of temples and triumphal arches shimmered frostily among the silver-gilt and porcelain.

Two half-starved kitchen maids were huddled in a corner, stuffing their mouths with candied plums and pigeon pie. A steward was quietly pocketing a fistful of silver spoons. Pattern ignored them all. She flung herself through the French doors and on to the balcony that ran the length of the room.

The moon was full but the balcony entirely dark, for the castle rose like a cliff above, cloaking it in shadow. Far below, a few fairy lights twinkled. And far ahead, across the wide lawns, deep in the woodland at the base of the mountains, was the quavering glow of torches.

She remembered Eleri's words:

Do you know what happens to princesses who are fed to the dragon? They are dressed all in white and led in solemn procession to a patch of wasteland, high in the mountains. And there they are chained to a rock, and left for the dragon to tear them to pieces . . .

Pattern doubted that Prince Leopold was a cold-blooded killer; in this respect, Madoc had probably spoken the truth. But what a fate, for Eleri to spend her whole life locked away in a lunatic asylum!

The Grand Duchess was reckless sometimes, hot-tempered too, yet always quick to acknowledge when she was wrong. For all the isolation of her status and upbringing, she was generous and warm-hearted – a Princess who had reached out in friendship to a servant girl. Pattern gripped the little pearl brooch all the harder. She was sure Eleri had the makings of a kind and wise ruler, if she was allowed to be. How frightened she must be now, how alone . . . And Pattern, who never cried, not since she was a baby, felt her cheek grow wet with tears.

Brusquely she dashed them away. This was not the time to indulge in weeping. She turned to where Dilys waited in the shadows, Franz by her side.

'So why aren't you part of the procession? Is it not one of Elffinberg's proudest traditions?'

'We're told the ritual is a holy thing,' Dilys replied hesitantly. 'A solemn pact between the people and the Crown. It is supposed to bind us together. But I've no stomach for it.'

'That's right.' Franz's jaw was set. 'They're a gang of ghouls, those folk who'd march Her Highness to her death. The same vultures who flock to public hangings.'

Pattern remembered the children's game of dragon-taming in the town gardens, and the girl who had played the Princess. How still and severe she had been, alone on her bench.

'What happens when they reach the mountain?'

'The Princess and her nearest male relation go on to the place of sacrifice alone,' Dilys explained. 'It's

forbidden for others to accompany them. There she will say her prayers, and be chained to the rock. And then she is left to her fate. The dragon always comes at dawn.'

'And the rest of the gathering?'

'They keep a vigil at the mountain's base.'

Pattern took a deep breath. 'I must go to her. I must stop this. Franz, will you take me?'

Dilys twisted her hands. 'There's a curse upon those who try and disrupt the ritual. It's against all the laws.'

'*This* ritual is false. Elffinberg is the victim of an elaborate fraud. The damage wreaked on the country has not been done by a dragon, but by Prince Leopold and his friends. You must believe me, and help prevent a very dreadful crime.'

Quickly Pattern related what she had found at Caer Grunwald, and the discoveries of the porcelain manufactory. Every second's delay brought Eleri closer to her doom, but she knew her story must be a convincing one.

'Gunpowder and fireworks!' exclaimed Dilys at the

end. 'Chinese potters! And those poor, dear captive children! How my blood boils to think of it.' She shook her head. 'I never cared for the Prince, but who'd have guessed he was such a fiend?'

'He's played us all for fools.' Franz snapped off a piece of sugar-paste temple and chomped on it disgustedly. 'And that's what we are, I suppose, for swallowing such lies and never questioning our masters.'

'So you'll take me to the place of sacrifice?'

He exchanged glances with Dilys. 'We'll do whatever you want. I reckon it was a good day for Elffinberg when you came home.'

Elffinberg? Her homeland? How strange to think of it at such a time! Yet until recently, Pattern would have thought it incredible to have made even one friend in the Duchy. Now she had three – and she intended to fight for them.

Chapter Twenty

*Consider and pause over the last scene of human existence –
a mournful and awful scene it is!*

J. Bulcock, *The Duties of a Lady's Maid*

Perhaps it was the headache, or a lingering grogginess from the drug, but Pattern had no plan of action and not the least idea of how to form one. So she went to find herself a weapon.

She had extravagant hopes of finding a pistol or sword hidden in Eleri's chamber, but the only armoury she could find was a poker from the fireplace. She supplemented this with the smelling salts and the remains of the laudanum sleeping tonic she had used to drug Lady Agatha. Finally she added a bottle of cleaning fluid she found on the backstairs. She was now equipped to send someone to sleep as well as wake them up, beat them off with a poker, and blind them with bleach. It was hard to envisage exactly how these actions would come about, but it was the best she could do.

After she had finished her search, the Grand Duchess's chamber looked as if a whirlwind had hit it. Pattern felt a pang of guilt for whoever would be tasked with the tidying if she did not return. Yet there was something oddly liberating about leaving a room in a worse state than she had found it. For the first time, she could understand Eleri's glee in smashing all that porcelain.

Franz's act of rebellion was to steal the best horse in the stables: Prince Leopold's new hunter, a glossy chestnut named Dragonfly. He said he'd had a great longing to ride the animal from the moment it was

first brought to the yard. There was nobody about to challenge them as he led it out of its stall.

Pattern had never been up close to a horse before, and would have been quite happy to keep things that way. She had no wish to get within striking distance of the animal's hoofs and teeth, and it was all she could do not to squeak as Franz swung her up on to the saddle behind him. The ground seemed very far away. 'Lord, doesn't Her Highness feed you none? You're light as a handkerchief.'

Dilys's eyes were dark and fearful, though she tried to smile as she waved them off. 'I knew you were trouble as soon as I laid eyes on you, Miss Pattern. First you entangle us in high treason, and now horse theft!' Then she caught at Pattern's foot, and said in a low voice so that Franz could not hear, 'Keep him safe. Promise me. *Promise.*'

They clattered out of the wide cobbled yard and round to the castle gardens, following the same route as the procession. It was tradition for the sacrificial maiden to travel to her doom in an open carriage, which moved at a walking pace, since everyone else was on foot. At least this gave Pattern and Franz the chance to catch up with the throng.

As Franz urged the horse from trot to canter and then gallop, Pattern clung to his waist and resisted the impulse to squeeze her eyes shut. As they sprang out of the tree-lined walkways and across the widening lawns, the horse's hoofs drummed on the dry earth, and warmly scented air blew in her face; the sky was bright and disordered with stars. Although they were riding into all kinds of danger, Pattern savoured the illusion of escape. Behind them lay the corrupt hulk of the castle; below, the spiked monster, coiled in its lair.

Their pace slowed as they reached the woodland, where Franz urged their mount through a rough but wide track through the gnarled trunks. The leafy canopy above was thinly speckled with moonlight; the darkness seemed full of strange rustles and snufflings. But it was not long before they saw lights through the trees and caught up with the stragglers at the tail end of the procession. It was a motley crowd, in which

ball guests in their silks and furs mingled with those servants who had lately waited on them, as well as the commoners who had gathered to protest outside the castle gates. Small children grizzled in their mothers' arms. There was little talk, save for the background murmur of whispered prayers, and the lilt of a doleful folk song.

Franz had to be quite forceful in pressing Dragonfly ahead, and compelling people to make way for them. He got some black looks, as well as indignant mutterings. Some deliberately tried to block his path. 'Have you no sense of decency?' several asked. 'Who do they think they are?' complained others. Finally they overtook the remainder of the procession and joined the many hundreds of people gathered on the lower slopes of the mountain side. Here a gloomy sort of campsite had been made. An air of weary dread, mingled with a strange suppressed excitement, hung over the scene. Several fires had been lit, even though the night was warm, and bread and cheese was being shared out. Fine ladies picnicked on the grass next to farmers with mud on their boots and straw in their hair. The melancholy folk singers – the song was about a lost maiden on a lonely hill – continued their dirge. Rival lamentation came from the ruins of a chapel, where a black-robed priest was conducting prayers.

The open carriage used to convey the Grand Duchess stood abandoned under a fringe of woodland. Franz reined in Dragonfly nearby.

'We won't get any further on horseback,' he said, dismounting in one smooth bound. He helped Pattern clamber down as best she could. 'The path to the place of sacrifice lies the other side of that chapel.'

'Thank you. I'll be quite all right from here.'

'You can't go on alone! I'm coming with you.'

Pattern thought of Dilys asking her to keep Franz safe. In her heart of hearts, she doubted very much that either she or Eleri was going to come back down from the mountain.

'There really is no need,' she said briskly, patting the carpet bag in which she had stowed the poker and her other particulars. 'I have a weapon to defend myself,

and a plan of action too.' It was still possible one might come to her. 'And – well – if it does not quite work out, it will be your task to convince people here of the truth. Besides,' she said, when Franz looked likely to protest, 'it will be easier for me to slip through to free Her Highness undetected than if you accompany me. I am much more used to making my way unnoticed.'

She smiled at him quickly, and turned to press through the crowd before she could think better of it. She had not got very far before somebody clutched her skirts. It was Lady Agatha Craddock, looking more iron-grey than ever in the shadows. Her voice dripped with satisfaction. 'Now you see, missy,' she hissed, 'that you are not the only one to be so cunning with your potions.'

Pattern shook her off in disgust. It was as she feared: even if she had felt able to rouse the people to action by explaining things as she had to Dilys and Franz, there were enough of Prince Leopold's agents about to silence her before she could even begin. And she had no time to waste. Dawn was approaching, and with it Eleri's hour of reckoning.

The chapel's tumbledown walls could not contain its congregation, which had spilt out all around. The priest was assisted by two yawning choirboys. His flock wept noisily over their candles and joined in the responses with all the fervour of the newly converted.

Pattern made her way through the quivering throng as unobtrusively as possible. Through the mossy ruins of the north transept she could see a stony path that zigzagged up between thorn bushes. Head down, she set off towards the slope. 'Where are you going, child?' called the priest, breaking off his Latin droning. 'That is holy ground, forbidden to the likes of you. Only the sanctified may walk on it. You risk both your life and your immortal soul!'

Several of the congregation made as if to go after her. But here the ancient superstitions of Elffinberg served her well. 'There's a curse upon that path,' one said to another, hanging back. 'Let her meet her own doom,' said someone else. 'Besides, the guards will turn her back.'

It did not surprise Pattern that there would be some sort of armed sentry in position. She reassured herself that they were unlikely to be expecting trouble. There were plenty of shrubs and bent crooked trees to provide cover; she must hope to hide in the darkness and so evade them. As she threaded her way through the scrub, the glow of candles and campfires already some way behind, she wondered how Eleri must have felt, stumbling in her thin silk slippers over the jagged stones. How long would the effects of the drug last? Would they numb her fear, or just her limbs?

Pattern found the sentries in a little hollow in the hillside. They wore the livery of Prince Leopold's personal guard, and she recognized one fearsome moustache as belonging to the man who had challenged her in Caer Grunwald. He would not challenge her now, however, for he and his companion were dead. They lay sprawled in the silvering light; the ground beneath them was clotted with blood. It seemed they had been felled by two blows to the head. Their weapons were gone.

The taste of sickness rose in Pattern's throat. But she could not afford an attack of the vapours. The gruesome sight must sharpen her wits, strengthen her resolve. These were Prince Leopold's people. Why had they been killed? Did he doubt their loyalty? Or did he not want to leave any witnesses to his crimes?

She gritted her teeth and inched forward, clutching the iron poker. The path widened into a clearing. There was an unmarked carriage standing by; it must have been brought up in secret by some other route, ready to spirit the Grand Duchess out of the country and into her prison. The horses blew their nostrils and stamped their feet skittishly; they seemed as nervous as Pattern.

Their driver sagged motionless over the reins. He, too, was someone she recognized: Howell, the coachman in league with Madoc, and another man who had paid for his treachery in blood. For several agonizing minutes Pattern waited in the shadows, hardly daring to breathe, watching and waiting for signs of ambush. Who else might be lurking here? Perhaps the priest was right, and there *was* a curse on everyone who took this path.

Then she heard a groan from within the carriage. Her heart jumped and stuttered. It took all the courage she possessed to go over and open the door. Prince Leopold was slumped across the seat inside, clutching his breast. Blood bubbled there darkly.

'Y-your Highness! Who has done this to you?'

He blinked at her blearily. 'You're the girl . . . the little maid . . .'

She hovered, undecided. Perhaps if she was to run back down the path, call for help . . .

But he reached out a clammy hand, clumsily beckoning her close.

'My . . . niece . . .' he rasped. 'You must go . . . go to her . . . Please.' The light in his eyes was already fading. 'Beware . . .'

One last bubbling sigh. Then he was gone.

Chapter Twenty-One

∽ ∾ ∽ ∾

Death, for aught you know, may, at this very moment, be on his way to you.

J. Bulcock, *The Duties of a Lady's Maid*

∽ ∾ ∽ ∾

Stowed under the seat of the bloodstained carriage was Pattern's sewing basket with its cache of documents. Rather than destroying the evidence, the Prince must have decided the papers were still of value. But they were of little use to anyone now.

The path narrowed as it climbed, and the scrub gave way to bare earth and stone. Although dawn had begun to show in the east, the sky seemed filled by the lowering darkness of the mountain. It seemed impossible that any living thing could be found on its silent, barren slopes. A chill little breeze had begun to blow.

Pattern was aware of how her heart pounded, and that sweat prickled icily at the back of her neck. Her breath was shallow and fast. She noted these signs with scientific detachment. In spite of everything, she was not about to succumb to a fainting fit; she had no need of a restorative sniff of the salts. A good servant was used to suppressing her natural instincts and emotions. A good servant always gritted her teeth and got the job done.

A *great* servant was master of her own destiny.

At last Pattern reached a narrow pass that led into a wide plateau. It was partially enclosed by spurs of rock, which formed a natural arena. Pattern crept through the shadows, crouching behind a thorn bush to survey the scene. To one side, a small white figure drooped in chains. Above her, the path continued upward, widening as it led into the blackly gaping mouth of a cave.

There was more. A stack of wooden kegs, metal cylinders and coiled fuses – Prince Leopold's Chinese explosives. A small fire, surrounded by an assortment of ritual objects. A tall man, feeding the flames.

Madoc. Pattern was not surprised. She had already guessed as much.

Peering through the half-light, Pattern thought she could make out three bowls made of crystal, gold and bone. There was a silver hand-bell and neat heaps of dried leaves, coloured powder, a couple of candles and something that might be a snakeskin. This last was guesswork, based on the illustration of the snake she had seen in the chapel fresco. Madoc was attempting whatever incantation Prince Elffin had used to bind the dragon to his will.

Murder was terrible, but it could be understood. Black magic was an unimaginable evil. Even with all that had happened, the hints she'd been given and whispers she'd heard, Pattern's common-sense mind shrank from the very idea of it. Yet in a country where young girls were routinely fed to dragons, who knew what other Dark Age barbarisms might linger?

At least Eleri was still alive. Although gagged, and bound in chains to a rocky outcrop, she struggled against her bonds as Madoc walked purposefully towards her, holding a long curved knife and the crystal bowl. He touched the point of the blade to her wrist. Eleri twitched away, and choked out a scream.

It was now or never. With sweating hands, Pattern raised the poker and got ready to charge . . .

Yet Eleri was not dead. Not yet. Madoc had made a slit in her wrist, but the cut was shallow. Pattern let out a long shaky breath as she watched him put the crystal bowl under her arm to collect the blood. Another part of the ritual, then.

Whatever the magic involved, it seemed complicated, and formed of several parts. Having collected blood from his captive, Madoc threw it on the fire, and circled the flames, chanting softly and ringing the bell. He looked as serenely efficient as if this sort of exercise was as normal a part of his routine as dressing his master for dinner. There was no hint of the murderous deeds

so lately committed. His cuffs were still white, his shoes immaculately polished, every perfect hair perfectly in place.

Now Madoc moved to the jutting edge of the plateau, facing east to where the horizon was rimmed with silver and primrose. He drew some kind of symbol or diagram in the dust, using the tip of the knife blade. Then he knelt in the centre of the diagram, arms uplifted, in salutation to the rising sun. His voice rose and throbbed; ancient Welsh tumbled from his mouth. From the increasingly triumphal sound, it was likely he was reaching the climax of his incantation. Behind him, the fire spat oily black sparks.

On tiptoe, skirts held up lest they should rustle on the ground, Pattern darted across to where Madoc babbled and swayed, and brought down the poker on the back of his head, letting out an indistinct but quite ferocious battle-cry as she did so.

He fell to the ground most gratifyingly. After a trembling moment, Pattern crouched down by the body and set about binding his wrists with strips of cotton torn from her petticoat. She felt calmer with something practical to do and, in spite of everything, relieved that the man was still breathing. After all, it would have been easy enough for Madoc to slip a knife into her ribs, back in the castle storeroom.

A search of his pockets yielded a rusty key. Pattern hastened to unlock her friend's chains.

At first, they had no words. The two girls simply clutched at each other, disbelieving and dizzy with relief. 'Oh, Pattern! I knew you would not forsake me. I *knew* it.' Eleri's face was blotched with tears, and her voice raw from strangled screams, but at least the numbing effects of the drug appeared to have worn off. Words now spilt out of her, uncontrollably. 'Madoc killed my uncle. And some other men, too – stone dead! I saw it all and could do nothing, and it was more shocking than you could imagine. Even worse, he knew all about the dragon! I can't think how. He was going to wake the beast up, and feed me to it so that its strength would be restored, and it would be able to do frightful things at his bidding.'

While she was still talking, Pattern – with some difficulty – dragged the unconscious valet towards the rock, and locked him into the same chains that had been lately used on his victim. She felt somewhat easier once this was done, but not entirely. She could not stop glancing at the gaping cave mouth above.

Eleri followed her gaze. 'Do you think it is too late, and the dragon has already been awakened?'

Her voice shook, so Pattern made sure her own was firm.

'Madoc is no sorcerer, let alone a dragon-tamer – merely a jingle-brained valet with ideas above his station. But you must go down to the people now. Franz is there, waiting. He will help you tell them what has happened, and why. You will find proof of the plot in your uncle's carriage. Then you must call the guard, and anyone else with weapons and authority, and find a way of putting an end to the dragon once and for all. Whatever it takes – poison gases or dynamite or bricking up all possible entrances to that cursed lair.'

'And . . . and what will you do?'

'I will follow presently. First, though, I am going to take your uncle's explosives and put them ready in the cave mouth.'

'But I thought you said Madoc couldn't—'

'Just in case, you understand.' She tried to smile. 'You know I do not like to leave anything untidy or incomplete. Now go. *Hurry*.'

Pattern might have imagined it, with all that was going on, but when she was tying Madoc's hands together with her torn petticoat, she had thought she felt a tremor in the ground.

She went back to the fire. It had nearly died out, but the precisely arranged objects around it struck her as highly sinister. Herbs smoked in the gold dish, and green powder fizzed in the bone one. What point had Madoc reached with his incantations? How far did his preparations go?

'I should have known it was a mistake to spare you. You're a crafty little thing.'

Madoc had recovered surprisingly quickly. He gave his chains a thoughtful tug and – wincing – drew

himself up so that he was sitting with his back to the rock.

Pattern ignored him. She picked up the first keg of gunpowder and began to roll it towards the cave.

'It won't help, you know,' he called after her. 'It's too late. The dragon is already on its way. Those firecrackers will inflict about as much damage as flea bites.'

'In that case, you'll be the creature's first victim.'

'Oh, I don't think so. It knows its master's voice.'

Pattern put the keg down on the path and came back to confront him. 'You're not even in control of your own wits. How can *you* be master of anything?'

'By virtue of my royal blood.' He gave an elegant shrug. 'It so happens,' he said casually, 'that I'm cousin to your precious Grand Duchess.'

'Pfff! This is just more evidence of your delusions.'

'On the contrary. It's a very common tale, my dear Miss Pattern.' There was blood in Madoc's hair and dust on his clothes, yet not a jot of his composure had left him. 'Common, sordid and sad. You see, the Grand Duchess's grandfather once took a liking to one of his maidservants. When she was found to be expecting a child, he had her thrown out of the castle like so much rubbish. The girl was barely sixteen. After giving birth to my mother, she died in a workhouse – the same workhouse I was raised in. All I have to show for my heritage is a little gold key my light-fingered granny managed to slip into her pockets just before she was booted out. Can you guess which door it opens?'

Pattern swallowed. She remembered the ancient chapel with its peeling frescoes, the wall of rock with its hidden catch. So Madoc, too, had followed the passage to see what nightmare festered in the castle's depths.

'I must have tried every lock in the castle before I found the fit. But those of us who must make our own way in the world are nothing if not resourceful. Patient, too. I'm sure *you* understand, Miss Pattern, being a penniless orphan yourself. As it happens, there are many advantages to being a self-educated man. So much knowledge has been forgotten, or else deemed too obscure for the modern schoolroom. My hours of scholarly isolation in the library proved most rewarding.

Do you remember how I told you to trust in the old tales of magic and adventure, of dungeons and duchesses and things that go bump in the night? Well, they led me to some very interesting alchemical research. It turns out that when science meets the supernatural, all kinds of miracles can be performed.'

'Your magic tricks are nothing but humbug,' Pattern said defiantly. 'They didn't work for Prince Elffin, and they won't save you.'

'Ah, but when Elffin Pendraig attempted the spell, he was sick and weak, and the dragon was strong – too strong for even the most powerful spell. Now the dragon is old, while I am young and vigorous. I have performed the ritual that will awaken the beast, and spoken the Words of Power that will give me its command. I will rule it, and ancient though it is, the creature will be quite deadly enough for my purposes. I will have at my beck and call the ultimate weapon of war. In early times, the people here worshipped it as a dark god, and they will learn to bow down before it again.'

He spoke quite matter-of-factly. Pattern was

conscious of another tremor in the ground; small pieces of grit shook free from the mountain slopes. Fear clenched around her heart. 'And this is why you pretended to help Prince Leopold?'

'Naturally. He would never have come up with such a plan on his own. The fat fool should have stuck to playing with his china teapots. But the buffoon wanted a shiny crown to prance about in, and who better to help him steal it than his loyal valet? No one so discreet, no one so devoted, so highly dependable! I even coaxed him into thinking he'd invented the plot himself.'

The valet licked his lips, and Pattern saw something strange. His tongue was long and black.

'And speaking of devoted . . . here you are: Pattern the loyal lapdog, always trotting after your mistress, faithfully wagging your tail as she shuts you out in the cold and the dark. She had no qualms, I see, about leaving you here, while she herself fled to safety.' His eyes shone hot yellow in the gloom.

'I told her to go. I *wanted* her to go.'

'Why waste your energy defending her? You are

twice as clever and capable as our glorious monarch, and you know it. Our so-called masters are fools and criminals. The old order needs to be overthrown.'

In spite of everything, Pattern laughed. 'You style yourself a revolutionary, yet you are every bit as greedy and corrupt as Leopold. At least the Prince was no murderer. At least he never wished to wage war on his own people.'

Her fury was so scorching that she almost forgot to be afraid. For it was not just Eleri she wished to save – it was Dilys and Franz and the castle's little scullery maids; the old women in the marketplace and the harvesters in Caer Grunwald . . . even the pimple-faced footman who had called her a mouse. Right then and there, Pattern had never felt more of an Elffishwoman.

Madoc shrugged. 'I have earned my place and proved my worth a hundred times over. I regret you don't see it that way, but it makes little odds, in the end.'

Then he stood up and carelessly snapped his iron chains in two.

Pattern froze. It was not possible. It couldn't be.

He stretched out his arms. From the tips of his fingers, hooked black claws were sprouting. 'Ha! What's this?' He regarded the claws in wonder, but without fear. 'Strange. There's a fire in my veins. I can feel it rising – the strength and heat of it, how it burns . . .' He laughed, and with mounting horror, Pattern saw his forked tongue flicker against yellow fangs. 'Sweet poison! Perhaps I misread the invocation. Perhaps I confused one part of the spell. It matters not – for it appears that I have gone one better than Prince Elffin. He only sought to rule the creature: *I* am going to become one with it. For now I too, Ferdinand Madoc, have become a creature of fire and frenzy and blood.'

Pattern turned on her heels and fled.

'Too late,' he exulted. 'Madoc's Bane has already risen!'

There was a rumble, like thunder, of grinding stones. Pattern was not far from the pass, and the downward path. But Madoc made a gesture with his clawed hand, and a bolt of lightening streaked down in front of her,

stopping her in her tracks. It left the ground charred and smoking.

'You will be my dragon's first victim. A gristly morsel of maidservant, to whet its appetite for the tender flesh of a Princess . . .' Suddenly he clutched his chest and staggered, gasping and groaning. Pattern felt a moment's hope. But the next instant he straightened up, standing impossibly tall, and his voice rang with even greater triumph. 'Ah – the magic has me in its grip. Now I can feel the beat of a second heart within me. I can taste the beast's hunger in my own mouth!'

Out of the cave, a sulphurous stench billowed, followed by a blast of hot air and ash. Loose rubble rained down from above. There was more grinding and creaking, and the grating of stones. The dragon was dragging itself up and out, towards the light.

When the ash cloud cleared, the creature was revealed to be even bigger than it had looked in its lair: the size of a house, or a hill. Many of its scales were broken and rusted. Its eyes were filmy. Its joints creaked. But it was still black and oily and serpentine,

shining with ancient malevolence. Slow and slithering, it crawled out to mount the ledge directly overlooking the plateau. As it flexed its leathery wings, and clashed its fangs, and let out the first great hissing roar, Pattern felt a fool for imagining bullets or even gunpowder could so much as dent its bulk.

She tried once more to move towards the pass. Another flash of lightning ripped and crackled through the air, and she was forced to jump back. Madoc's transformation was more hideous by the moment. His

clothing split as his body rippled and bulged; greasy black scales had begun to shimmer over his skin. His shoulders split into bladed spikes; his eyes were slits of flame. He saluted his monster, and his cry of welcome – hoarse and croaking – was more beast than man.

The dragon was changing too. Its own eyes were rounder, less snake-like; there was a trace of aniseed in the rotten fumes of its breath. As it turned its horned head towards Pattern, licking its rusty jaws, the sound it made was unmistakably human. A deep, low chuckle. She had heard it before: in her and Eleri's dreams.

'Pattern! No!'

Eleri came panting and skidding through the pass.

'What are you doing?' Pattern shouted. 'Go back! Run, while you still can!'

'I heard the dragon. I couldn't leave you to face it alone!'

She looked up and saw Elffin's Bane awake and risen for the first time. Already pale, her face drained of all colour. Her mouth gaped and knees buckled.

The thing that had been Madoc flung out a clawed hand to shoot a fire-bolt in Eleri's direction. This roused her from her stupor, at least, for at the last possible moment she managed to dive out of the way. With a scream of defiance, she lunged towards the dragon.

Pattern leaped after her and dragged her into the temporary shelter provided by a pile of fallen rocks.

'Let me *go*.' Eleri struggled furiously against her grip. 'I'm what it wants. If it takes me, then maybe it will spare everyone else.'

'Wait. The dragon and Madoc have become one and the same. Do you understand me? *They are the same thing.*'

'How does that help us?'

'If we can disable Madoc, then that will injure the dragon too!'

Both girls yelped. A bolt of lightning had ripped into the rocks in front of them, blasting a chunk of their shelter into shards. Pattern, grimly brushing dust off her hair, hunkered down to search her bag, which

she had somehow managed to hold on to through the scrimmage.

Eleri spied the disinfectant and gave a hysterical laugh. 'This is no time for housework!'

Pattern was too distracted to reply. She opened the cap on the smelling salts, releasing vapours of ammonia that made her eyes prickle, and hastily poured the crystals into the bottle of cleaning fluid labelled 'Chloride of Lime'. The fumes increased in sharpness, making her cough. For good measure, she tipped the laudanum sleeping tonic into the brew. It was Madoc's ritual arrangements that had given her the idea – she was no magician, but Mrs Minchin's Academy had at least schooled her in the hazards of domestic cleaning solutions, as well as the chemical make-up of medicinal aids.

Another streak of fire smashed into the rocks. Devilish laughter echoed all about. They were now utterly exposed, with nowhere to run, nowhere to hide. Madoc and his monster were playing with them like cat and mouse.

The dragon drew back its head, snorted smoke and sparks, and prepared to strike.

The Madoc-creature gave another croaking chuckle.

And Pattern flung the bottle of chemicals at his face.

She did not expect it to disable him for more than a few moments. Her hope – and it was a desperate one – was that the dragon, too, would momentarily be stopped in its tracks, giving Eleri and her one last chance to flee through the pass. And if Madoc had simply dashed the bottle away, or even let it crash upon his person, this hope would have most likely been in vain. Instead, he aimed to shoot the missile down in flames.

The moment the lightning bolt flashed from his scaly palm and hit the bottle, the sky exploded. The force of it flung Eleri and Pattern backwards as broiling flames gobbled through the air, swallowing Madoc in their white heat. At the same instant, the dragon let out an anguished scream that was horribly human in its despair. The world was consumed by choking stink, and bitter smoke, and the crackle of greedy flame.

*

Dust and ashes. Two corpses.

The remains of a man with the skin of a snake, burnt almost beyond recognition.

A smoking heap of prehistoric bone, already beginning its long decay into the mountainside.

Two friends, walking hand in hand over stones, in the morning light.

Chapter Twenty-Two

Go where you will; the character which you have made for yourself will be certain, sooner or later, to follow you.

J. Bulcock, *The Duties of a Lady's Maid*

Pattern Pendragon, Countess of Annwn, High Commander of the House of Elffin, Dame of the Order of the Purple Daffodil, was having a perplexing morning.

She had arrived in London in a wintry fog, which had now turned to rain. Fog still appeared to hang within the airless offices of the Elffish Consulate off

Bedford Square, to which Pattern had come in an effort to discover more about the identity of her parents. The consul, a portly gentleman whose fondness for cigars was the chief reason for the murk that clouded his office, had been roused to great heights of energy and attentiveness by the letter of royal instruction sent ahead of Pattern. But he warned her – between puffs on his cigar – that the likelihood of uncovering reliable information was slim. Although the Grand Duchy's border authorities kept records of those persons who had 'unlawfully absconded from Elffinberg', the file for the year of her family's departure had been lost in an archive fire.

Pattern had been spurred on her quest by witnessing the release of the stolen children of Elffinberg. Having been hustled away from Prince Leopold's manufactory, they were found locked in the extensive cellars below his hunting lodge. Amid the rejoicing of their parents, the happy tears and tender embraces, Pattern felt an ache all of her own. Her family could never be reunited in this life; the least she could do was try and learn their names.

The consul had one possible lead. He had unearthed a letter sent to his predecessor by an Elffish clergyman, in which the writer mentioned that his mother's favourite pastry-cook had lately vanished, along with his wife and infant daughter: '. . . *I suspect they have taken fright at the notion of the Old Trouble returning, and so have chosen to take their chances in exile instead. If you were to hear of any Elffish arrivals in London, I should be very glad to be notified . . .*'

The letter was dated the same year and season as the shipwreck in which Pattern's mother and father had perished; the surviving crew members had confirmed that she had been the only infant on board. As far as evidence went, it was extremely feeble. But Pattern remembered her stolen holiday in Elffinheim, where the spice of gingerbread had been her first taste of freedom. I should have liked parents who were pastry-cooks, she thought. I hope they exchanged proof of their devotion in frangipane hearts, and wrote their affection in butter frosting. I hope I was born into a cloud of icing sugar and confectioner's cream.

Since she planned to stay in town a couple of days longer, she resolved to distract herself with sightseeing. She was a lady of leisure, after all. She had taken rooms in one of Mayfair's grandest hotels. Her stockings were silk and her shoes were of the softest kid. Her coat was of fine-combed wool. But her dress was as simple as it ever was, her demeanour as mousy, and none of the Londoners hurrying to get out of the wet and dirt gave her more than a second's glance as they jostled past.

However, she was not entirely unobserved. A grandmotherly-looking person was sheltering in the same portico that Pattern had chosen to take cover from the rain, and had watched her keenly as she emerged from the Consulate across the road.

'Miss Pattern?'

'Can I help you?' Pattern replied, trying to conceal her surprise.

'I hope you will forgive the imposition. I have a slight association with your former tutor, Mrs Minchin, and so thought I would take the liberty of introducing myself. My name is Adele Jervis, and I am the representative of a highly select employment registry.'

Pattern remained perplexed as to how she had been recognized, but she did not wish to appear ungracious. 'Thank you for your interest, but I am not seeking a position at this particular time.'

In fact, Pattern had no need to work for a living ever again. On her return to Elffinberg, she would have a spacious apartment in the castle, her own retinue of servants and a pension for life. Dilys and Franz had also been generously rewarded for their loyalty.

Mrs Jervis smiled. 'I am sure life in the Grand Duchy keeps you agreeably occupied. In fact, it is on Elffish matters that I was hoping you would do us the honour of a consultation. One of our new recruits served at the Elffish court, and though her references are uniformly excellent, we know little of employment practices there.'

Pattern looked at her carefully. The woman was respectably dressed, and had a naturally pleasant expression. Why should she not give her the benefit of her advice? She had nothing better to do. What's

more, the rain had suddenly been overtaken by pale December sunshine, which provided her with sufficient encouragement to shake out her umbrella, and follow her new acquaintance down the street.

They stopped outside a narrow stucco-fronted building, whose shining windowpanes and gleaming doorstep bore testimony to the value of good housekeeping. There was no sign on the door. Once inside, Mrs Jervis showed her into a well-appointed and airy office, where a man introduced as Mr Crichton was waiting. He was tall and silvery, with the air of unassailable dignity present in all the best butlers.

'My dear Miss Pattern,' he said, warmly taking her by the hand before showing her into a seat. 'It is a great pleasure – indeed, honour – to meet you at last. We have, as they say, been following your career with interest. Interest and excitement!'

Pattern returned his smile cautiously. 'I find that hard to believe, for I lead a very quiet life. I am not the kind of person exciting things happen to.'

'Our sources report otherwise.'

She lifted her brow. 'They must be extremely well placed.'

'We flatter ourselves that we have eyes and ears in all the royal courts worth mentioning, as well as in the highest households in the land. Which is how we came to hear of your defeat of Elffin's Bane. It is not often that one meets a lady's maid turned dragon-slayer.'

This time, Pattern could not hide her consternation. Although Eleri had been most anxious that Pattern should share in the passionate acclaim that had greeted her, following the death of the monster, Pattern had insisted that nobody should know of the part she had played. Moreover, she could not imagine how news of the dragon had got out, given the Duchy's closed borders and secretive character. Even its closest neighbours were unaware of recent events.

She endeavoured to keep her voice level. 'Whatever do you know about that?'

'No more than the bare bones of the matter. We would, of course, be very interested in hearing your own account, Miss Pattern.' He paused. 'Unless, of course,

you would prefer to be addressed by your proper name. Miss Pattern *Pendragon*, is it not?'

Pattern was yet more surprised. This had been Eleri's idea, and she was still getting accustomed to it. 'Pattern,' the Grand Duchess had said, not long before she left for London, 'you have made your name your own, and I should not like to ever call you anything else. So I have another thought. You remember that Prince Elffin called himself Pendraig, which is Welsh for "Chief Dragon". Well, I think *you* are the true chief, since you are the only person who ever bested it. And that is why Pendraig – or Pendragon, in the English form – would be a most excellent surname for you.'

This was not at all what Pattern had imagined when she had first thought to choose her own name. Eleri saw her hesitate.

'Dearest Pattern, you must recollect that in the ordinary course of things, you would have been given your name by your family. Neither of us has a mama or papa, but in you I have found a sister, as well as a friend. So perhaps you can look on Pendragon as a family name after all.'

Remembering this brought an almost painful warmth to her heart. 'Plain Pattern is how I generally prefer to be known,' she managed to say to Mr Crichton, though she was all astonishment.

Mr Crichton regarded her benevolently. 'Please don't be alarmed – you may have been brought here on false pretences, but rest assured the cause is a good one. Let me explain myself. We are an employment registry for domestic servants, that is true, but our staff provide a peculiarly specialist service. Elffinberg is not the only country with secrets and burdens. It is not the only corner of the world where strange relics of ancient times still linger, or where people have fallen prey to the Darkest of the Dark Arts.'

Pattern felt like someone who is trying to read a book when the pages are being turned a little too quickly. 'I'm afraid I don't quite follow . . .'

'The perfect servant is the invisible one. Invisible, incorruptible. Don't you agree? A trusted servant has

access to their employer's most intimate areas of life and work. A clever servant can turn this access to great advantage. And so our agency places servants within households for the purposes of discreet investigation. I have here, for example, a letter from a most noble lady, of great rank and wealth, who suspects her stepdaughter of summoning a demon to possess her. She implores our help, and offers ample reward. She may be a crank, of course. But she may not. What then?'

Pattern blinked. 'You wish me to aid such an investigation?'

'A girl of your talents and resourcefulness cannot sit idle for long.'

'The Grand Duchess relies on me.'

'The Grand Duchess does not need you. She will not be of age for some years to come. In the meantime, she does not lack support or advice. I hear she has already recalled her father's friends who were exiled or imprisoned by Prince Leopold, and restored them to their former positions on the Council of State. Both you and your former mistress are free to live a life of leisure, in luxury.'

'You speak as if that's a bad thing.'

'I certainly don't mean it that way. Why bother to earn your own wage, when you have a friend who will pay for your every particular? I am sure you will not want for anything in Elffinberg. Now that it has got over its fright, the Duchy will doubtless be as pleasant, prosperous and dull a backwater as anyone could wish. But – forgive me – perhaps you will indulge my curiosity on this one point. How *did* you slay your dragon, Miss Pattern?'

'It is a little complicated. But in essence the beast and its master were consumed by a chemical fire, triggered by a tincture of sal volatile, laudanum and, er, bleach.'

'Very neat! Very neat indeed.' Mr Crichton nodded approvingly. 'Ammonia from the smelling salts . . . chloride in the cleaning fluid . . . mixed together to produce a toxic gas . . . the ethanol in the laudanum provided the flammable element, I presume? And all

sourced from innocent domestic supplies! I must be sure to tell Mrs Jervis. Such information could be of great advantage to our operatives.'

'I had no idea it would be so effective,' Pattern admitted. 'And of course I was improvising. Now, if one were to experiment in properly controlled conditions, and allow for . . .' She caught herself. 'But that is not my concern.'

He smiled smoothly. 'Well, well, there it is. I regret that our work holds no appeal, but your reluctance is entirely understandable. Allow me to give you this, at least.' Mr Crichton passed her a card bearing an address, and the illustration of a feather duster crossed

with a toasting fork. Above this was the name *The Silver Service*. 'In case you have any further questions, you understand.'

Pattern felt it would be impolite to refuse the card. She bade Mr Crichton and Mrs Jervis good day and went out in the street, where the sun peeped in and out from rain clouds, and jewelled the puddles with a passing sparkle.

The afternoon stretched before her. She was entirely at liberty. She could eat as much gingerbread and lemonade as she liked. She could shop for fur-lined gloves and lace handkerchiefs. She could spend all evening at the theatre and all day at the museums. She could go to the pond in the park, and throw iced buns for the ducks to eat.

Or she could return to a life of drudgery and dirt and danger. Excitement and exhaustion. Trial and challenge.

It was time for her to choose the heroine she wished to be. She could be Countess of Annwn or plain Pattern . . . but not both.

And standing there in the chasing sunshine and shadows, she found herself wondering how one would go about banishing demons, and whether a poker or well-sharpened knitting needle would provide adequate defence.

Turn the page for an exciting
extract from Pattern's next
A Silver Service Mystery . . .

THE LOST
ISLAND

The journey from London to Cornwall felt nearly as long and arduous to Pattern as that of London to Elffinberg, not least because she had to make it in public stagecoaches instead of a private carriage, and under the watchful eye of Mrs Robinson. When she and the other maidservants finally arrived at the fishing village from where they were to take the four-mile boat journey to Cull, Pattern was so cramped and stiff she felt she would almost be glad to get back to scrubbing grates and mopping floors.

Elsie had not stopped chattering since they had left London. Everything was new, everything was of

interest. Pattern had sympathy for this – she had been just as wide-eyed on *her* first escape from the city. However, she had kept her astonishment to herself. Elsie could not pass sight of a cow, or a stream, or a picturesque cottage without remarking on it, and the moment she and the other maids caught sight of the sea there was such a hubbub as would deafen even the noisiest gull. Not even Mrs Robinson's sternest admonishments could silence them.

It was not the best of days for a visit to the coast. The fog seemed to have followed them from London, and everything was dank and dripping, and smelling of fish. Pattern, already somewhat sick from the jolting of the coach, looked at the choppy grey expanse of water and felt queasier still. She reflected that the Service had been advised that Cull was a craggy and desolate place. The two fishermen who were to ferry them over would only shrug in response to Pattern's enquiries about the island's history.

'Loss,' was all the older one would volunteer.

'Who is lost?' she asked. His accent was so thick,

and his manner so brusque, she feared she had misheard him.

'Cull. 'Tis from the Cornish for loss.'

The Isle of Loss . . . This did not bode well. Pattern was not fanciful, but she shivered all the same.

Yet when the shores of Cull first rose out of the mist, Pattern gaped in admiration just like the other girls. Although the island's cliffs were rocky, they were fringed thickly by trees, and the cove they were approaching glittered with white sand. The waves that lapped the island were a deep blue-green, not grey.

Except, that is, for the sea immediately ahead of their vessel. Pattern thought the black mass beneath the water must be submerged rocks, but then the darkness moved, passing under the boat like an underwater shadow. A few dirty bubbles rose to the surface. Nobody else had noticed it, and Pattern herself could not be sure of what she had seen.

Then all at once the last of the clouds parted and the sun blazed through, so that the scene was bathed in golden light, and the remaining mist that

enveloped the isle was transformed into a sparkling, shimmering haze.

The fishermen drew the boat up to a stone pier and helped them disembark on to the landing platform at the end. An old man, swathed in a billowing black cloak, was waiting to receive them at the top of the steps.

'My name is Glaucus Grey and I am the steward of this isle. On behalf of Lady Hawk, I am pleased to welcome you to Cull.' He gave a stiff little bow. Some of the more impertinent maids smirked. He had bristly white eyebrows, a wild white mane of hair and a face that was exceedingly knobbly. But he hobbled across the beach very briskly indeed, and as they lugged their baggage up the rough steps cut into the cliff face, it proved quite a struggle to keep up with him.

At the top of the steps, Pattern paused to take a breath. When she glanced back, she saw the boat that had brought them was already swallowed up by mist. Yet the sun continued to shine on Cull as the party followed a path through a wood. On the other side of a narrow though not particularly deep ravine was a sheltered glade dappled with snowdrops.

Elsie, naturally, had to stop and stare. 'What pretty flowers! Like little stars!'

'The local name for them is the moly flower, but they're for looking at, no more,' cautioned the steward. 'That side of the wood is dangerous and strictly out of bounds.'

Mrs Robinson peered across. 'But it looks such a charming spot.'

The old man grunted. 'You've heard of the Cornish adder, perhaps. Well, the Cull viper is its more vicious cousin. It nests up here, in that very glade, and a bite from its fangs is fatal. So keep your distance.'

After this warning, all were relieved to leave the wood. Emerging from the trees, they beheld an arcaded villa set against the hill. It was classical in style, with ice-cream-pale-yellow walls and a roof of terracotta tiles. A wide lawn in front of the house gave way to a formal garden whose beds were worked

into patterns of stars, half-moons and mathematical symbols, wound about with white pebble paths. Statues of nymphs and satyrs peeped out from a tangle of rose bushes.

There was no sign of groundsmen or gardeners and the place was silent apart from the drone of bees and the sigh of the sea. Even the chattering maids were quiet, too overwhelmed to do anything but stare. As the visitors made their way through the grounds, it felt as if the villa and landscape were half asleep, lying there drugged in the spring sunshine.

'Gracious!' exclaimed Mrs Robinson, surveying the orchard. 'Are those *lemon* trees?'

Mr Grey smiled. 'Cull's positioning is geographically unique. Thanks to a most favourable union of winds and tides, the climate here is considerably warmer and drier than anywhere on the mainland.'

'I see,' Mrs Robinson said rather faintly. 'Am I to understand, Mr, er, Grey, that you have sole charge of the property in Lady Hawk's absence?'

'That is so. I have been in service to my Lady for

so many years I can hardly remember a time I wasn't.'

'And no one else lives on the island?'

'Folk from the village make the crossing to tend to the estate and deliver such produce we cannot supply ourselves, but none are resident unless stranded here by bad weather.'

'But are there really no other servants? I was under the impression that casual staff would be engaged—'

'My Lady is quite content that you will be up to the job.'

Mrs Robinson pursed her lips. The maids exchanged grimaces. Fifteen servants was a large establishment for a town house. But in a country villa of this size, with a large party of guests to look after, they would be sorely stretched.

The aged steward led them through a sunken walled garden, richly scented with herbs, and from there to the service quarters. The rooms were large and echoing, with plaster peeling from the walls, and windows so overgrown with creepers that the place was bathed in a green underwater light. In the

servants' hall, a bare lofty room with a tiled floor, they were met by Mr Perk, the butler, who had come ahead with Mrs Palfrey and the other domestics and was doing his best to act as if he had had charge of the property his entire working life.

The sleepy silence of the place was soon overwhelmed by noise and bustle. Rooms must be aired, fires laid and beds made, and the contents of cabinets, closets and pantries explored. It was heartening to find that the house, though unlived in for so long, was in excellent order. Mr Grey had previously arranged for provisions to be brought to the island by boat, and the larder was as well stocked as the wine cellar. The meat safe, coal-hole and icehouse were all packed to bursting. Everything from shoe polish to sealing wax was in its proper place.

Lady Hawk and her daughter would be arriving on the morrow, the rest of the party the day after. As Pattern set about beating carpets, she rehearsed the visitors in her head.

The most eligible of Miss Hawk's suitors was Lord

Frederick Crawly, heir to a vast estate in Norfolk. His friend and rival, Captain Henry Vyne, was known as the handsomest man in England – and the best card-player in his regiment. The Reverend Anthony Blunt was more of a catch than most young clergymen, thanks to his aristocratic connections and the patronage of his uncle, the Archbishop of Barnchester. The final suitor was a poet, Thomas Ladlaw, who had been favoured by very complimentary notices in the *London Poetical Review*. His fortunes had further improved with a publication of a novel in the Gothic style, *The Towers of Viagrio*.

So much was public knowledge. The Silver Service, however, had been able to dig a little deeper, thanks to its information network of well-placed servants. These sources reported that Lord Crawly had been involved in the death of an old woman on his estate, though the matter had been hushed up and the circumstances remained vague. Captain Vyne left a string of broken hearts in his wake, and was rumoured to have fathered two illegitimate children. The Reverend Blunt had

stolen from a charity he himself had established for the relief of widows and orphans. Only the poet appeared clear of wrongdoing.

The ladies, by contrast, were as bland as they were blameless. They were comprised of society favourites Alicia and Adelaide Grant, their aunt the Dowager Lady Maude, Anthony Blunt's sister Honoria and her companion Marian Smith, a poor relation.

Pattern not only had to acquaint herself with the honoured guests, but the servants they would bring with them – the Grant sisters had a lady's maid and so did their aunt, and Lord Crawly would be accompanied by his valet. However, since these servants would be mixing with their fellows below stairs, getting to know them would be easy enough. Pattern's focus must be the gentlemen. The lord, the soldier, the priest and the poet . . . Such different professions and personalities, united only in their passionate desire to win Miss Hawk's hand! She wondered how the other young ladies would feel, being little more than accessories to the main purpose of the gathering. It could give rise to a certain amount of tension and resentment, she imagined. But then, Miss Hawk could only marry *one* gentleman. The disappointed suitors might well seek consolation elsewhere . . .

At three o'clock sharp the servantry gathered at the main entrance to the villa, forming a reception line to greet their employer. Only Mr Grey was absent. They were wearing their expensive new livery and arrayed in order of their station. Mr Perk had inspected them three times over to ensure not one hair was out of place, not one button done crooked, not one smudge to be seen upon a shoe. A peacock strutted across the lawn, its silken plumage shining azure and purple, as if in rebuke to the dull black and white row of humans in front of it.

A few minutes later, James the coachman could be seen driving the carriage along the winding avenue. (The mistress and her guests would not take the woodland path from the beach, but travel along a more formal road that displayed the island's views to

best advantage.) Mr Perk hastened to assist the lady and her daughter down from their vehicle. 'Welcome to Cull, milady.' He proceeded to escort Lady Hawk down the line of servants, in the manner of two generals inspecting the troops.

Lady Hawk had words of greeting for the senior staff, and a gracious smile and a nod for everyone else. She was tall and handsome, with a high arched nose and great quantity of inky black hair. Her complexion was enlivened by a pair of brilliant dark eyes and a full red mouth. The contrast to her daughter was striking. Miss Hawk was, indeed, a perfect English rose, as pale and dainty as her mother was bold and dark. She glided behind her with downcast eyes and a sweetly bland expression, holding a little pug dog in her arms.

The lady's maid, Miss Jenks, waited by the carriage. She was an elegant young person with a haughty expression, and dressed so finely she hardly looked like a servant. Even so, Pattern knew it was in her interests to befriend her. A lady's maid was often a repository of her mistress's secrets, as Pattern herself could attest, and even if Miss Jenks had only been with Lady Hawk for a short while, she was in a uniquely intimate position. Then there was Glaucus Grey, the only person to have been in the lady's employ for longer than a few months. He, at least, must know something of her history . . .

Pattern's thoughts were running on so busily it took a moment to realize that Lady Hawk had stopped in front of her.

'Now, here's a face I do not recognize.'

Pattern bobbed a curtsy. 'Please, milady, I am new to the position. My name is Penny, milady.'

Mrs Robinson stepped forward to explain the original third housemaid's desertion.

'Penny, you say?' Lady Hawk smiled. She had the merest trace of a foreign accent. 'So which of your parents enjoyed a classical education?'

'I – um – I'm sorry, milady, I don't quite—'

'Never mind, child. I'm only teasing. Perhaps you have not heard of the original Penelope: the long-suffering wife of that rascal Odysseus.'

'No, milady.' Pattern had had very little formal education at all, least of all a classical one, though she had endeavoured to make up for this by close study of the *Encyclopaedia Britannica*. She had chosen 'Penny' because it was a shortened form of both Penelope and Pendragon, her newly acquired surname.

Fortunately Lady Hawk did not pursue the subject. 'Well, I hope you will be happy with us, little Penelope.' She raised her voice to address the rest of the servants. 'Indeed, I hope you will all be happy here. A gathering such as this is hard work for everyone, I know. But I am sure we will show our guests every hospitality. They have been chosen with care and I am determined to give them exactly what they deserve, for my island is a special place. A sacred spot! Serve it well, and it shall reward you.'

It was a somewhat eccentric speech. But Lady Hawk was a somewhat eccentric employer, and her servants thought none the worse of her for it. The good order of the house and the comfort of their own quarters had done much to raise their spirits. From the light-hearted chatter that followed the inspection, Pattern realized she was alone in thinking that Lady Hawk's promise to give her guests 'exactly what they deserve' could conceal, perhaps, a note of threat.

The Mistress of Cull might describe it as a sacred spot, but the isle was certainly a very curious one. After all, Pattern reflected, there could not be many woods in England that were both blessed with snowdrops out of season *and* infested with snakes.

Acknowledgements

The author wishes to convey her esteem for the indomitable Miss Julia Churchill of A. M. Heath, as well as those keen-eyed and quick-witted ladies at Macmillan Publishers, Miss Lucy Pearse and Miss Rachel Kellehar. Good books, like households, require both ornamentation and orderliness; the former was provided by Miss Sarah Gibb, the latter by Mr Nick de Somogyi and Miss Veronica Lyons.

Especial gratitude is due to Ali Korotana Esquire, of Camberwell. It is to him that this book is most affectionately dedicated.

ABOUT THE AUTHOR

Laura Powell, who may or may not be a direct descendant of King Arthur, was born in London, but grew up in the shadow of Carreg Cennen Castle in Wales. Much of her childhood was either spent with her nose in a book, or plotting to escape her hated boarding school. Having studied Classics at university, she now spends her time working for the English National Ballet and writing. She lives in Camberwell with her husband and young son.

ABOUT THE ILLUSTRATOR

Sarah Gibb is a London-based illustrator. After landing regular spots in the *Telegraph* and *Elle* magazine, Sarah has gone on to illustrate Sue Townsend's Adrian Mole series, many classic children's fairy tales, and even the Harrods Christmas window display.